THE ACTIVIST PREACHER

Parts of this material published under title:
Beyond the Next Mountain

THE ACTIVIST PREACHER

Philip M Makau

Revised 2022

In memory of Reverend Gideon M. e'Thathi, whose life gave birth to the original idea for this book.

My deeply felt gratitude goes to Geraldine Erickson for her editorial comments which helped clarify much of the prose.

CHARACTERS

Gideon King'ele e'Muthembwa (*Reverend*)

Kanini – *the preacher's wife*

Matthew Muthembwa – *first son of the preacher and Kanini*

Joe Mutunga Muthembwa – *2nd son of the preacher and Kanini*

Esther Ndoti Muthembwa – *daughter of the preacher and Kanini*

Munyalo – *herdsman, neighbor of King'oo*

King'oo – *cattleman and wealthy landowner*

Kaveke – *beautiful youngest wife of King'oo*

Sue Gilchrist – *wife of Mutunga, works in Nairobi UNESCO office*

Nyamai – *promising young college graduate in Nairobi*

Dr. Wambua Itumo – *son of church education committee chair*

Dr. Nzungo Itumo – *younger brother of Wambua*

Priscilla Katee – *daughter of church deacon*

Samuel Kimweli – *agricultural inspector in the provincial office*

Bernadette – *scheming woman; mother of Christopher*

NOTE: In Kenya, many people are known by only one name, which is usually their African given name. During baptism they may acquire a Christian (non-African) name. They often use both names interchangeably. For all cases in the story, the last name is the equivalent of family name in the western world.

PROLOGUE

EARLY IN THE twentieth century when the British colo-
nized Kenya, they gerrymandered the country into
provinces which they then carved along tribal lines
into administrative units referred to simply as "districts." A
British commissioner headed each district and in turn created
smaller administrative units known as "locations." He made
lifetime appointments of local Africans to administer each
location at his pleasure; he could fire any and all at will. The
Africans designated as administrators of these locations were
called "chiefs" and functioned as direct agents of the
government in their locations. They maintained the spirit of
loyalty to the British Crown and inculcated such spirit. They
had the responsibility of collecting taxes and of seeing to it
that the African inhabitants in their locations obeyed all
lawful orders.

The immediate effect of this partition was the confine-
ment of tribes within their ancestral areas and the discour-

agement of inter-tribal migration, thus limiting commu-
nication between the tribes. Partition was accompanied by
registration of all African males, sixteen years and up, for tax
purposes and one could obtain the obligatory identity card
only in one's tribal district. Any man caught not carrying an
identity card faced dire consequences: jail and a beating or
worse. Your location of origin established your official resi-
dence, regardless of where you actually lived or worked.

The obsequious and often pompous African chiefs from
the local area who administered each location with its sub-
locations tended to pander to their British masters and to see
to their own personal interests rather than to those of the
community. They wielded enormous power over the ordinary
citizen since they had the authority to determine how much
one paid in taxes, bequeath unclaimed land to whomever
they chose to favor or appropriate the acreage for themselves
if they so wished. Many were thoroughly corrupt and corre-
spondingly resented. It is no wonder, then, that many of them
met an ignominious end during the turbulent struggle for
political independence. During the colonial era however, the
chief was the person to have in one's circle of friends if one
wanted anything done within the locational boundaries or
beyond. The location chief was the ordinary citizen's conduit
to any available government services and the ubiquitous
bureaucracy.

King'ele, a personage who was to powerfully influence
the destiny of his people, came on the scene during this era.

ONE

NO ONE KNOWS exactly when he was born, up on the hills of Kilungu in Ukambani. It is said that when the railway came, King'ele son of Muthembwa, was already a young boy. By such calculations he would have been born between 1890 and 1894, the third oldest of four siblings. He was of medium build and height, about five feet eight inches.

Early in his life, he became aware that the family did not have much in the way of traditional wealth. He realized that by the time his parents paid bride price for his two older brothers there would be little left for him when his time to marry came around because most of the disposable cattle and goats would be gone. To improve his chances of being able to pay bride price for *his* future wife he made up his mind to look elsewhere. His spirit of adventure and curiosity about the world beyond the horizon undoubtedly contributed to this decision.

Of the four siblings, he was the first to leave his Kamba home out in the rural area of Kenya to look for work in the nearest white settler farm. At the time, there were no cities in Kenya; former rail construction depots were just beginning to grow into hamlets. Nairobi, the largest depot, was then a large town surrounded by white settler farms. Illiterate, King'ele could only find employment as a manual laborer, a coffee bean picker on a white settler's plantation. Kenyan plantations of the era were similar to company towns in that the workers lived on the plantation and were dependent on the farmer for food, shelter, and all necessities of life. Workers tried to save the pittance they earned to send home and in any case, it was not sufficient to buy anything in the nearest town.

King'ele's lack of literacy did not daunt him because he was ready and willing to improve his lot even if it meant starting with the most menial work. Some of the employees at the farm were Christians from the Kikuyu tribe who, after work, taught their compatriots how to read and write as they introduced them to the new religion, Christianity. Always eager to learn new things, he soon was able to read, write, and thus follow the Bible stories. He recognized literacy as a means of improving his chances for a better paying job while religion gave him the peace of mind he yearned for.

King'ele was soon promoted to supervisor as he was a hard worker and the white coffee farmer recognized his determination and leadership qualities. The possibility that he might also have ideas of his own about running the plantation did not occur to the farmer since it was a widely accepted belief that Africans were only capable of taking orders but not of taking initiative. King'ele, on the other hand, had great confidence in his ability to size up a problematic situation and think of ways to improve it. Thus, circumstances dictated that a clash was inevitable.

Every day one or more of the workers fainted during work in the field and one day Thiongo, one of his most diligent and trusted workers staggered and fell. King'ele went over and asked him what was wrong. Thiongo did not want to answer at first and turned his head away, but when King'ele insisted, he said,

"Sir, I am hesitant to tell you, but I am weak from only getting two half-gourdfuls of maize meal all day."

That was about two cups of maize flour per diem.

"Why did you not tell me earlier?" King'ele asked.

"The last person we asked to speak to the supervisor for more food was punished by being denied food for one day," Thiongo explained.

King'ele decided that for the number of hours they were out picking coffee beans the workers needed more nourishment so he told Thiongo,

"Don't worry, you will not be punished. I'll see what I can do about it."

King'ele called upon traditional wisdom to decide what needed to be done, saying to himself, "A herdsman does not starve his cows if he wants to get a full gourd of milk." As supervisor, one of his responsibilities was to distribute food to the rest of the employees so he decided to remedy the situation, an act that put him on a collision course with their hard-nosed employer.

"Who authorized the increase in food rations?" demanded the irate British farmer when King'ele went to request additional maize meal.

"I noticed the workers were slowing down because of hunger. Therefore, as supervisor, I decided to remedy the situation. As you can see, sir, everyone is happier and picking beans faster. There'll be more coffee bags at the end of the day," King'ele replied, his self-confidence daring the farmer to contradict him.

"Your job is to distribute the amount of food I authorize. Tomorrow I expect you to reduce the ration. I will dock the cost of the extra food you gave from your pay. Is that clear?"

"But, the amount you have been feeding them isn't adequate," King'ele protested. His sense of fairness would not allow him to back down.

"I'll brook no interference by any of my employees," declared the settler, giving the young man a withering glare. King'ele stared back without flinching. "You're fired. Leave my farm *now*," the farmer ordered.

He did not wait for any owed wages. Quietly, with his dignity intact and without any apology for his action, King'ele left that plantation to seek similar employment on a sisal plantation at the opposite end of town. He knew what was fair and no one was going to tell him otherwise. The young man also knew that by slightly increasing the amount of food for the workers the farmer would more than break even when the additional bags of coffee beans were sold.

A few days earlier the supervisor at the sisal plantation had fallen ill and returned to his tribal area to consult with the witchdoctor so the owner was delighted to have an experienced and competent replacement. While working there King'ele entered into a "come-we-stay" marriage with a woman from a different tribe, an inter-tribal arrangement that was very rare at the time. Customarily, if a man lived with a woman in the same hut for a week they were considered married and thereafter the man was expected to pay bride price to the woman's parents.

One day King'ele came home from work to find his house emptied out: his wife had packed everything that indicated anyone ever lived there and disappeared back to her tribal home. That was the final straw; he had enough of inter-tribal marriages and living in town. The sudden end of his brief marriage made him rethink his departure from his tribal roots. That night he left with the few belongings he had brought from his work, never to return to town life. His sojourn into urban life beyond the tribal borders left King'ele disillusioned about that lifestyle.

Nonetheless, his contact with the outside world had introduced him to Christianity, a western religion unfamiliar to his people. When he returned to his parents' home, they were not pleased with this development.

"How can you defy tradition and customs? It is sure to lead to isolation and disaster," they warned.

Regardless of his parents' displeasure, their disapproval did not deter King'ele from acquiring better reading and writing skills from a nearby missionary school. He was determined to make sense out of the Bible and understand this new religion better. That the new religion forbade drinking alcoholic beverages did not make him hesitate in embracing it. For the rest of his life he forswore partaking of any drink that contained alcohol.

Understanding the white missionaries was not without awkward and at times funny moments. Few of the foreigners mastered the local language; they learnt it as they preached and few ever acquired full fluency. Learning a tonal language was a new experience for them; they would often fail to hear the right inflection and therefore end up saying something entirely different from what they intended.

One missionary young King'ele came into contact with

always talked about the birth of Christ a long 'bone' ago. However, the worst was when, in his booming and emphatic voice, the missionary declared to the assembled congregation that Christ was 'sodomized' on the cross instead of being crucified. Explanation of this shocking statement required many private talks with leaders in the congregation on how to undo the damage done by this sermon, as it had made some wonder about the new religion.

King'ele had saved some of his earnings from his work on the sisal plantation but the money was hardly enough to buy the necessary number of cattle and goats for bride price. Quick to notice an opportunity, he soon offered to help around the missionary station as an apprentice mason and carpenter in constructing more buildings at the mission settlement. Through these skills, he was able to save enough to make a down payment towards his future wife's bride price.

When he had saved enough for a decent down payment he began looking around and thinking seriously about what kind of wife he wanted. He did not want to be fooled again by attraction to a stranger he knew nothing about. Since there were no Christian single women in the community, he did not feel guilty courting a non-Christian girl of his tribe.

He had seen a pretty girl herding goats in a field not far from his parents' place and on inquiry found out that her name was Kanini. He saw her again at the spring where families in the area went to get water and managed to get past her shyness to have a short conversation. Her soft voice and sweet demeanor pleased him greatly, so he asked his parents to make the traditional overtures to her family for her marriage. They were happy to do so, knowing she was from a good family and had a reputation for stability and hard work. The ritual negotiations went well and he built a hut for her on a plot next to his parents' homestead shortly before they were joined according to customary law. Soon thereafter their marriage she became a believer in Christ. They became devoted spouses and years later, before starting his missionary work in far places, they would renew their vows in a Christian ceremony. His second and final wife became a powerful influence in his life and work.

King'ele, or e'Muthembwa, as every adult male of a certain age and social standing in the community was respectfully called, employed his newly acquired literacy to found a local school while he and Kanini were raising their first child. He built a hut that served as both a schoolhouse and a church, then recruited students from his own family and the neighborhood and hired a teacher. He became the school administrator, boarding subsequent teachers in the home he shared with Kanini and supervising them as well as making sure students showed up for classes. This was his idea of improving the community.

The year he started the school and church, Kanini and e'Muthembwa's younger brother were among the new students. Three years later, his first child was enrolled in the same school. His wife had quit a few months into her schooling because she objected to the teacher's way of disciplining: he had struck her hand so ferociously with a stick that he broke a bone in one of her fingers. Shortly after the incident, e'Muthembwa busied himself looking for a better teacher.

Concurrently, he was wooing European missionaries to adopt his school and church. At the end of the third year after the school and church opened their doors they became mission-sponsored institutions. When the missionaries took over they told him that he needed to be trained if he wanted to become a proper preacher.

As part of the training, he had to be baptized, thus affirming his conversion to Christianity. He knew that during baptism one walked into the river to be dunked but did not realize that during the ceremony he was supposed to choose a Christian name. On the day of his baptism e'Muthembwa walked down from his house through the reeds to the bank of the pool of water in the river. There he patiently waited for the rest of the converts to assemble and the white minister to arrive. To make sure he was the first to be dunked he waded in.

Just before he pushed King'ele into the water the minister asked,

"E'Muthembwa, by what name shall you be known?"

"King'ele son of Muthembwa," he replied, humbly omitting the honorary 'e', which means 'son of' and is bestowed upon sons after they attain a traditionally prescribed level of respectability.

"That's not enough. You need a Christian name," said the minister.

"Why? Everybody knows me by those two names."

"You must have a name from the Bible. Hurry up and choose! We don't have all day for one convert. You don't have the faith of Gideon." (In the Old Testament Gideon prayed for the sun to stop in the sky so that the Israelites could finish fighting their enemy.)

"Oh, but I do."

"Then from henceforth you'll be known as Gideon King'ele son of Muthembwa," said the minister as he dunked the new convert.

It was a fitting name for an unrelenting activist. Could

this simple man from "upcountry" also be a visionary who
would be a major force in the spread of literacy and Christianity in Kenya?

E'Muthembwa's sermons were unique: instead of the
common, puritanical fire and brimstone if one did not
convert to Christianity, his were uplifting. He rarely raised
his strong and steady voice, but spoke quietly and reassuringly. With an unwavering gaze, his brown eyes would fix
one congregant and then another, always making each one
feel included. The sermons often used traditional storytell-
ing. In a culture rich in proverbs he employed many in his
effort to make sure the congregation understood the Christian
message immediately.

Once, in explaining that God does things at His own
pace, the preacher used the Kamba proverb: *Kukalaata utuku
tikw'o kukya* (To hurry the night does not bring dawn
sooner.) His preaching advocated living a good, honest life,
devoid of sloth and mindful of other people's needs. Such
sermons made sense to anyone who hoped to live a produc-
tive and worthwhile life. In truth, they did not present any
substantial conflict with the traditional values of his people.

As part of his ministry training, he learnt to read musical
notation in tonic sol-fa for leading church hymns. Even
though he had minimal music training, with his keen musical
ear and tonal acuity he could hit any note with perfect pitch,
including sharps and flats while singing *a cappella* in a
strong, clear tenor voice. One could always pick out his
voice in any congregation. This was a great drawing card for
a people who have a naturally tonal language and love to

11

sing.

Before starting his training for the ministry, he was already planning to improve the school and church buildings. He had picked the high ridge above his house as the site of the new church, where he would position the building so that its windows faced north and south. Such a plan would allow even natural lighting to come in during services. From the house on a hill, as he called it, the wind would carry the voices of people praising God far and wide, a sort of indirect advertising.

He organized the community to collect materials and provide manual labor. He donated the lumber which he and a friend had hand hewn. Under his leadership, wooden molds were hammered together to make bricks which he stacked and fired. By the second year of his training and with the community's help, this man of few words had built two new structures, one for school and the other for the church. The two buildings were no more than rectangular clay brick and mud wall, grass thatch huts with open windows. Modest though they were, the new buildings were sturdier structures, a sign to the community that education and religion were there to stay.

The tools he used for building marked the beginning of his homemade carpenter's shop, a clearing under a Brazilian pepper tree. He fashioned a workbench that was supported at one end by a post dug into the ground and at the other was nailed to the tree. The big tree also provided shade as well as a place to hang his tools when he was not using them. He crafted most of the tools in his shop himself; they were a hodge-podge of functional but simple, rudimentary pieces.

He did not rely on his preaching stipend to support his family of four but combined his preaching with other activities, such as farming, fabricating and laying bricks, and carpentry. In addition to produce gleaned from the small farm he and his wife owned, he was able to augment the family larder by buying things with earnings from building houses and selling doors or windows he made in his home shop under the pepper tree.

Over time, he became a forceful leader of both community and church. As the congregation grew, civic leaders were amazed and wondered how he had done it. They asked him to organize the people to participate in land reclamation projects – such as planting ground cover on barren areas and digging catchments to slow water drainage down the denuded hillsides.

The end of his ministerial training found King'ele determinedly organizing the larger community to increase school enrolment and church attendance. At the same time, he was introducing new ways of using the land. The area was hilly and the traditional methods of farming encouraged soil erosion. He was the first in his community to terrace his field and apply cow manure before planting the next crop. It was not long after this that others started copying him. By then he was into crop rotation and putting sections of his small parcel of land on fallow.

The leaders at the mission headquarters also noticed his success and leadership. They had planned to expand the reach of their mission work to other areas so they started posting him to new places to put up church buildings and nurture new congregations. As soon as the new church was up and running, they would transfer him to another place, to repeat the same "miracle." For several years, he was the roving preacher: get there, build a church, establish a reasonable congregation, and then move on. With his woodworking, brick making and building savvy as well as his feel for leadership, he became a trailblazer for the dissemination of Christianity.

Having to move every few years took a toll on his parenting; he simply did not have time to deal with his first son's school problems. Over the years, he traveled to various places while his wife and children lived near his parents. E'Muthembwa yearned to see his own family more frequently and told the church leaders so, hoping they would leave him in peace at his original church but that was not to be.

One day he was called to the mission headquarters where the director announced, "We have a special mission for you far away beyond the next mountain. We need you to hold together the congregation in the land where the baobab tree grows, in Kithongoto, until we find a permanent preacher. The religious landscape there is as barren as the land around the baobabs and we think you are the one person who can pull together the few congregants remaining after the last preacher left. Would you do it for just four months while we search for a permanent replacement?"

Several preachers had been sent to Kithongoto, the farthest church from the white missionary headquarters. E'Muthembwa knew that within a short time each had succumbed to the pleasures of the flesh. The last preacher posted there had gone native, ceased preaching or attending any service, taken a second wife and built himself a house far away from the church! It was said that the people in that area were too free in expressing their sexuality, which, according to the Christian belief, made them loose and immoral people in dire need of salvation, much like the biblical inhabitants of Sodom and Gomorrah. No one wanted to be the preacher appointed to lead that congregation. The missionaries could not think of anyone else resilient and dedicated enough to tackle the problems at Kithongoto.

Never one to shy away from a challenge, one to whom failure was no option, E'Muthembwa said, "Yes, I will even do it for six months instead of four." He knew his reputation was on the line and that his faith was going to be tested as at no other time. In his heart, he was sure that in the end he would prevail but just how he was going to do it was not so clear. He had faith combined with common sense and believed that self-reliance was necessary if he was going to succeed in his new mission. Like the biblical St. Paul, e'Muthembwa believed the Lord would not give him a burden too heavy for him to carry. With a heavy heart, he once more bade Kanini and the children farewell and left them behind to start his three-day trek through dangerous bush country to the new posting.

The first thing he did when he got to Kithongoto was to acquire and clear a small piece of land and plant crops for his own food. Next, he asked his home mission for funds to build his own house, a modified two-room mud hut with a corrugated roof, not far from the fairly modern church with its brick walls and steep corrugated roof. Contrary to tradition and unlike most men in the area, e'Muthembwa had learnt how to take care of himself: he could cook his own meals, wash his own clothes and in essence manage his own house. All the while, he was cautiously establishing friendships with the local leaders in order to gauge the mood of the community.

Few in the community recognized that the new preacher was different from the last one who had arrived expecting the congregation to take care of his daily needs. Nevertheless, many expected the new one to fail just like all his predecessors. Many watched and waited for e'Muthembwa to stray from the holy path. Various female members of the congregation insisted on wanting to cook and keep house for him. He politely but firmly discouraged them because he did not want temptation that close. The most he allowed was for them to fetch water from the well for him, a chore he made sure they did while he was engaged somewhere else, away from the house. They did not understand how a man could live alone for months without female company. Unfounded rumors began to circulate that he was one of those who hated women because there was something physically wrong with him or was gay. If they could not get him one way, they were surely going to get e'Muthembwa in another.

Nothing worked.

What they did not reckon with was his absolute resolve that he was going to turn that congregation into a thriving church. Almost four months after his arrival e'Muthembwa had won over a few key supporters. Among them was the local chief who gave him land, separate from the church property. Hoping that the new preacher's interests were as worldly as his predecessors were, the chief also invited e'Muthembwa to be a key member of the local administrator's governing committee and thus co-opt his talents in the chief's own schemes.

The alert preacher's focus never wavered; instead, he saw this as an opportunity to reach even more people and thus increase the size of his congregation. To each new acquaintance, he extended friendship and a dose of Christianity. By this approach, the preacher added several new converts to the growing congregation, including the chief who became a fervent supporter of the church after his baptism.

Two

UNYALO WAS BORN into a poor family in the hills surrounding the village of Kithongoto. His father did not have as many head of cattle or goats as his neighbors. In fact, other than a couple of milk cows and several goats he had nothing compared to King'oo, his next-door neighbor whose herd was so large that when some of his cattle did not come home for the night he hardly noticed. It was a good thing that the community watched out for one another: King'oo's stray animals were always herded back to his homestead by caring neighbors. That was the traditional and right thing to do, take care of your neighbor and he will do the same for you.

In a culture in which one could marry as many wives as one could afford to pay bride price for, King'oo had seven, a reflection of his wealth and status. Each wife, with the exception of the youngest who shared a hut with the first wife, had her own hut. The nubile young woman he married last was almost twenty years younger than his oldest son.

When he married her, it was more a statement of his wealth rather than any interest the decrepit old man had in her as a wife. King'oo was past the age of being able to have sex. Poor Kaveke was simply an addition to her husband's possessions, something to look at and for others to lust after and nothing else. She had been married off to the old man by her family because King'oo offered the highest bride price for her outstanding beauty. Besides, every family was loathe to be stuck with an unmarried daughter in the family and Kaveke's wanted the most they could get for their astonishingly beautiful young child. Being almost fifteen, she was considered 'an old maid' in a tribe where most girls were married off before they reached twelve.

All such a young wife could expect was a life of indentured servitude to the first wife and to be provided for by her husband. In return she was expected to remain faithful to her non-performing husband, to remain chaste the rest of her life. This only added to this young teen-age wife's frustration. She envied her friends who had handsome young husbands and wondered what it was like to enjoy making love the way they described it.

It did not take long before Munyalo noticed the stunning addition next door. He wished his family were well off enough to afford what he imagined to be the bride price paid for the beauty across the acacia thorn fence. Even though she set his loins on fire, he knew it was not only dangerous but also useless to dwell on the thought. His family could not come close to matching half of the cattle and goats King'oo had paid for her and he vaguely knew that customary law had dire sanctions against any man taking another's wife.

Furthermore, tradition demanded that a curse be pronounced on the homestead in which the wife had been seduced. The feelings aroused in him by the sight of Kaveke made him even more determined to get married as soon as his family got enough for a down payment on bride price but he was at a loss as to how they were going to get more live-stock for such a payment.

Then the idea hit him: he would hire himself out to herd King'oo's large herd of cattle, if the old man was amenable to the idea. He knew that his neighbor had gone through several herdsmen whom King'oo had found wanting and that at the time two of his sons were grudgingly looking after the cattle. With his father acting as his emissary, Munyalo offered his services for two heifers every rainy season, a total of four every year since there were two wet seasons in the year. The astute old man thought it a bargain and hired Munyalo; he had watched his neighbor's son grow up and knew he could trust him to do the best with the herd. He identified two calves as the herdsman's first payment at the end of the coming rainy season. The arrangement was now complete.

By the end of the second year, Munyalo had eleven head of cattle – four cows, four heifers, two calves and a bullock. He was happily looking forward to his next payment. The next rains were due in less than a month, when he would stop having to move the herd over long distances looking for water and forage.

Then providence intervened. He had led the herd to the well when he came face to face with Kaveke. The inter-vening years had been generous to her looks. Her stunning beauty, which she was all too eager to flaunt, had matured. Munyalo could only guess since he had never seen her close. Now he marveled at the fine features of her face, compli-

21

mented by wide-set, almond-shaped eyes with thick curled lashes, all held in place by a slender neck. Her soft lips parted in a self-conscious, dimpled smile to reveal an even set of white teeth. The traditional cloth she wore covered only one shoulder, revealing the base of her firm, young breast on the opposite side. The feminine shoulders atop a straight back that flared into full hips below the leather thong that secured the cloth around Kaveke's hips sexually aroused him.

Their eyes locked ever so briefly. Kaveke let out a coy giggle and looked away as she stepped aside to let Munyalo walk past her. She had noticed him from a distance a few days after he started herding for her husband and wondered whether his strong and sensual physique had an equally attractive face. Now she knew, for what he lacked in material wealth nature had compensated Munyalo in looks. He had a smooth, chocolaty, unmarked skin and a body any woman would yearn to caress. His eyes were kind and seemed to invite her to caress his body. As Kaveke walked away she stole a glance back at him. "I wonder how it would feel to be in his arms," she thought, but immediately pushed the thought away.

If he had not noticed other neighborhood wives heading his way the young herdsman would have loved to stare at the departing, swaying hips but he knew better. Although he went about his business as if nothing had happened, Munyalo could not get his heart to slow down. Kaveke had stirred emotions in him that his twenty year-old mind said were dangerous but he could not banish them. In fact, he thought about his neighbor's wife late into the night and into the following days. He could not get her out of his mind. He dreaded the consequences of such thoughts even as he unthinkingly began scheming ways in which he could run into Kaveke again. He now wished the rains would hold off a little longer; then he would have a better chance of seeing her close when she went to fetch water at the well. He was too inexperienced to know whether what he felt was love or lust. From his peers, he had heard details about sexual intercourse; they however, had not dwelt on wanting to spend time with a woman.

Munyalo was not the only one having such thoughts because Kaveke's mind was in a tizzy with fear and excitement. Thoughts of the herdsman made her heart beat faster, her knees weak. Her eyes scanned the scrubland near the horizon daily for the herd movements, trying to time her trips to the well to coincide with their watering time. Such a plan, she thought, would make her own trips less suspicious if anyone was keeping an eye on her.

A week into her new routine King'oo's first wife asked Kaveke,

"Why have you stopped using the larger gourd? It is not too heavy and you won't have to go for water so often. You've been preparing meals later than usual. You're getting lazy!"

"I'm sorry, mother (as she always referred to the first wife). I'll do better tomorrow," Kaveke reassured her.

The following day the dry hot winds had ceased, heavy clouds in the tropical sky indicated that it would not be long before the rains started. Kaveke took the larger gourd to the well but before she got there she used a sharp stone to puncture a small hole near its bottom. She stuffed dry grass in the hole, filled the gourd with water, slung it on her back and headed back to the hut. On arrival "mother" noticed her wet back.

"I guess that old thing is cracked. Let us hope the rains will be plentiful this season. That ought to give us time to grow another gourd," she observed.

Kaveke smiled to herself but said nothing. Her plan was working even though she had not succeeded in meeting Munyalo again. She was beginning to lose hope because the rains were getting closer than ever and the young herdsman had taken to driving the herd farther away in order to make sure the animals were getting enough feed to sustain them through the dry season. The dry scrubland could yield only sparse brown stubs of dry grass, so Munyalo had changed his routine, grazing the herd for two or three days before bringing the animals back to the well instead of bringing them back every day.

The fateful day started with the smell of rain in the air, overcast with ominous dark clouds. The dust devils from the previous day had died down to be replaced by still, muggy and heavy air. The ground was ready for a good, heavy downpour but by late that afternoon, no rain had come. By now, the herd was due back at the well, a large open reservoir in the dried riverbed.

In the meantime, Kaveke was getting anxious since time was running out. She knew that as soon as the rains started her chances of running into the young herdsman at the well would diminish. She was not sure what she would do if they met again; she just had an irrational urge to see him at all costs. He had not brought the cattle for water for three days and so she kept a watchful eye out for dust clouds in the distance, a sign that the herd was on its way to the well. She busied herself at the hut she shared with the first wife as she bade her time.

A few hours before sundown, Kaveke saw in the

distance what she had been waiting for, the telltale wisps of dust. She hadn't started out earlier because she did not want to have to wait for Munyalo at the well and thus cause the first wife to become suspicious. She knew that if she waited a few more minutes she would beat the herd to the well, thus assuring herself a gourd full of un-muddied water but Kaveke could hardly wait. Her excitement barely registered with "mother" who attributed it to youthful energy. After stalling around awhile to give the herd time to get closer, she set out for the well to fetch water, the last woman on that day to go to the well.

She had just finished filling up the gourd when the first wave of cattle in the large herd arrived. She looked up and saw Munyalo standing a few yards away, quietly watching her. Her heart missed a beat as she swallowed hard. The clouds were thickening, giving the day an appearance of later hours. She heaved the full gourd onto her back and slowly walked a few yards in the opposite direction from the path she normally took back to the hut. Munyalo could hardly believe his good fortune; his hormones took over from his brain as he moved to intercept her path. As he got closer to her, his heart was pounding with excitement and, he noticed, his palms were sweaty. All he could think of was his desire to possess her.

By the time he reached where she was, Kaveke had put the gourd down and sat on the ground behind a thorny shrub, hidden from the well, waiting. With her knees drawn up, the red-brown cotton cloth she wore secured around her young waist fell away to reveal smooth, strong and shapely thighs. Seeing this tableau drove him to the brink. Munyalo simultaneously threw down his herding stick and the plaid quarter cloth he had draped over his broad shoulders. He loosened the brown skimpy loincloth he wore and knelt in front of Kaveke, hands on her raised knees.

Months of yearning, dreaming and anticipation were rolled into that moment.

"Do you remember the last time we met?" Munyalo asked nervously.

"How could I forget? I knew as soon as you started working for the old man," Kaveke responded.

"Really?"

"Of course!" said Kaveke, coyly looking skyward and rolling her eyes.

Their eyes were locked, searching each other's face, uncertain of how to proceed. She reached forward and pulled him by the shoulders. As she did so her body continued to fall backward forcing Munyalo to support his weight on his elbows. Awkwardly but gently, the two virgins found their way. Their sexual appetites satiated they disentangled and self-consciously smiled at each other. Silently, Kaveke picked up the full gourd, slung it onto her back and headed for home, her thighs slightly stiff and her face beaming in the semi-darkness of the early evening.

The satiated cattle had been ready for rest after quenching their thirst and had settled down to chew their cuds. Munyalo picked up his discarded garments, put on his loincloth, all the while relishing his good fortune. Now more than ever, he wished Kaveke were his wife.

That night the rains came as Kaveke slept, content and happy that she had finally lost her virginity to the man she desired and no one, other than the two of them, was any wiser.

With the rains having started there were other sources of water and the herd did not have to come to the well. She longed for Munyalo but knew the chances of meeting him again were almost nonexistent until the next dry season – four or so months in the future. So, she buried her thoughts in the routine of the household and waited for the season to change.

THREE

BOUT A MONTH later, Kaveke started feeling weird since she could not understand why she was the only one getting sick when she ate the same food everyone else did. Sometimes she would get sick on an empty stomach. Then it hit her: she was pregnant, a fact that was not lost on the first wife.

"Mother" watched carefully as the pregnancy progressed. She knew her husband was not responsible for it; furthermore, it was unimaginable that any of his sons would have dared touch their stepmother. The first wife suspected the young herdsman but knew her young co-wife would never own up to who the guilty one was. Kaveke had wrought the most heinous traditional transgression and a curse on King'oo's household and somehow the truth had to be forced out of her. Only then would the person responsible for her pregnancy be brought before the *king'ole* (the elders' council) and made to atone for his treachery and thus the

29

curse would be exorcised.

The first wife secretly embarked on convening the traditional female inquisition group. Only women with grown children were included in this hard-nosed *ngolano*. All were beyond childbearing age, strong and evil looking. They set a day and a time when they knew they would trap Kaveke in the hut she shared with the first wife. On the chosen day "mother" sat at the only exit from the smoke stained hut as the old women quietly gathered in a neighbor's hut. They picked a leader and as they emerged from the igloo-shaped grass hut they broke into a chant-dance, moving as if they were possessed. The sight and sound was enough to make all the young women in the entire village tremble with fear. Each listened fearfully to the old women's vicious chant, hoping she was not the object of their derision.

"Where does the fig tree grow?" the leader yelled.

"In Kaveke's vagina," the others chorused back.

"Where does the grass grow?" she shouted.

"In Kaveke's twat," they answered.

"Who has the moldiest womanhood?"

"Kaveke has the rotten vagina."

A few other descriptive questions and answers were shouted, all intended to be heard by the entire community, including the target of their insults.

Seated inside the first wife's hut, at first Kaveke could not believe her ears. Then she looked at the first wife and froze. She knew the jig was up, that "mother" had discovered the pregnancy. "Mother" had planted herself just inside the hut exit with a look on her face that dared the young woman to try to make a run for it. A whimper escaped from Kaveke's mouth. She could now hear clearly every word the group leader shouted. The insults had moved to all the traditionally loathed wild animals, the carrion eaters.

"Who would bed a hyena?"

"Nobody else, but Kaveke."

The *ngolano* was now at the gate to the homestead kraal and getting closer. Kaveke's body had an involuntary shiver as if a freezing gust of wind had blown past her. She had heard vague stories about errant wives being punished by the *ngolano* and that the experience was terrible. No one ever detailed these experiences for her. The women were outside the hut when they changed from the question and answer routine to song as they continued dancing wildly.

"I need a thousand men to satisfy me,

If I can't get a man, I'll bed a donkey.

If I can't get a man I'll bed a … (names of different animals called out.)

Oh yes, I'll bed anything with a penis."

Then they delivered the *coup de grâce*. With the loudest voice the old woman could marshal, the leader asked her final question,

"Have you heard who's got the largest twat?"

"Nobody can challenge Kaveke. She'll take on an elephant!" responded the chorus with equal enthusiasm.

By now Kaveke's reaction had changed from being mortified to being petrified. Her breathing had turned shallow and her mouth was dry. Although she tried to focus she could only see a blurred outline of the first wife. Were they going to cut the baby out, mutilate her genitals or in some other way scar her body?

The group outside became silent as two shadows darkened the hut exit. Two heavy set old women with bare drooping flat breasts and knee-length brown cloths fastened around their waists moved deliberately to where Kaveke was sitting with her back against one of the posts supporting the roof of the smoke stained hut. Unceremoniously, the two dark shadows seized her by the arms and hoisted her up, in almost the same gesture stripping her naked to reveal a young body showing early signs of pregnancy. Unnoticed by Kaveke, a third ominous looking figure had come into the darkened hut with something in her hands.

The first two women retrieved ropes from under their garments and tied Kaveke's wrists together and around the support against which she had been leaning. As they let go, the young woman's knees buckled but her tied wrists supported her weight. The third woman smeared her entire naked body with ghee, liberally covering Kaveke's private parts. With the exception of her head, every part of her body, including the soles of her feet, was greased. She wondered whether they were planning to beat her to within an inch of her life. The three silent old women then turned and exited the hut, to be replaced by two others who entered bearing kindling in their arms.

Quietly they approached the dying embers in the hearth and started rekindling the fire, all the while adding more wood until the flames were about a foot high. Kaveke's fat smeared body was beginning to sweat from both fear and the heat. The fire stokers too retreated outside without a word being spoken. First wife maintained her glaring sphinx guard at the hut entrance. Kaveke remained in a trance-like state, aware of what was going on but attaching no specific meaning to it.

Then a third wave; two unsmiling, bare-breasted, old women, entered the hut, each carrying an unlit grease-soaked torch. The look in their eyes brought Kaveke back to the present. Their expression signaled they were not to be trifled with. Kaveke was now sweating profusely from the fat smeared on her body and the heat from the blazing fire. The older of the two new arrivals slowly walked to the fire to light her torch. Then she turned and stared at the shiny, naked young female body as she approached Kaveke with the flaming torch held horizontally and away from the side of her half-naked body, an evil smile on her face. Suddenly her straight arm came forward and up, bringing up the flaming torch, slightly singeing Kaveke's pubic hair. The young woman closed her eyes and held her breath in anticipation of pain, but none came. She opened her eyes to find an eyeball right in front of her nose.

"The next one will be closer," hissed the old harridan. "Who is the baby's father?"

Kaveke wanted to speak but words did not form in her head and her mouth was parched dry. If she had been a cat her eyes would have been all black with fear. She noticed the second woman had lit her torch and was approaching. Kaveke let out an involuntary scream but no one seemed to notice. A foot from Kaveke's face, the second woman stopped and eyed the young woman's calves.

"Who is your baby's father?" she demanded.

For a split second, Kaveke hesitated and the flame moved to within two inches from her shiny calves. Before she could summon enough strength to utter his name, the flames licked her lower legs, enough to cause burn blisters. The terrified young woman had never experienced such intense pain before.

"Speak! If you thought that was painful wait until you have to give birth," said the torchbearer in a tone full of menace and satisfaction. "Who is the father?" she demanded.

"M-m-munyalo," stuttered Kaveke.

At that moment Kaveke saw something in the older woman's right hand reflect the light from the torch flames. She struggled to focus and realized the old woman had a knife. She sensed a sudden and involuntary contraction in her abdomen as nausea overcame her. "This is the end for me," Kaveke thought as she fainted.

"Enough!" commanded the first wife, suddenly coming to life. The old woman with the knife reached up and cut the ropes off Kaveke's wrists and helped cushion her weight as the young woman's body collapsed to the floor. She then helped the first wife put Kaveke's limp body onto a dry cowhide that was next to where the young woman had been suspended.

That evening the first wife relayed to King'oo, her husband of many years, the information the *ngolano* had extracted from Kaveke. The old women had done their part, what remained now was for the *king'ole* to even out the score. Traditionally, information obtained through the *ngolano* was not challenged.

Shortly after dawn the following day, the humiliated King'oo sent word to Munyalo's father that he wanted to have a meeting with him. Normally the two did not have much to do with each other, so the young herdsman's father was curious about the proposed meeting. He wondered whether his neighbor was going to suggest a better deal for his son. When they met in the afternoon, Munyalo's father could hardly believe what King'oo was telling him: how could his only son be so foolish? How dare he shame his family by disturbing the peace in the home of the most respected man in their neighborhood and his benefactor?

He agreed that the *king'ole,* a council to which only the revered old, married men who already had children of their own were invited, should meet and implored King'oo not to demand that Munyalo be banished. In a society in which if the community did not know all the generations from your great, great grandfather you were considered a stranger and an enemy to be hunted down like a wild animal, banishment was synonymous with a death sentence. It was one of two choices the men's council could make regarding any single man caught having sex with his neighbor's wife. King'oo agreed to punish the errant herdsman, instead of banishing him.

Word was sent to fathers of young men of Munyalo's age group in the community and a date was set. As was customary, Munyalo's father set about making the traditional brew to be consumed during the tribunal and informed his son that his herding duties were terminated as he had agreed with King'oo.

"I want to hear it from you. Did you have sex with King'oo's young wife?" Munyalo's father demanded.

Munyalo was stunned. He did not comprehend how his father could possibly know about his secret tryst with Ka-veke and briefly considered answering evasively. His hesitation caused a stern outburst from his normally soft-spoken father, "I already know the truth, so don't lie to me, boy!"

"Yes, father, I did, but it was only once," Munyalo answered guiltily.

"You fool! That's all it takes. What were you thinking?" he asked in anguished disappointment, not expecting his son to answer. "I have to let the *king'ole* decide what punishment to give you. You must promise me never to go near that woman again."

"I promise, father," Munyalo answered with sincere determination, not imagining that he would ever have reason to

35

go back on his word.

"You're expected to provide a bull for the council to eat during your trial," the father informed his son. Munyalo was crushed by this news.

The *king'ole* expected Munyalo to sacrifice his only bull for the elders' feast. A bull was called for and no other animal would do. It was a painful punishment for the young herdsman to give up his soon-to-be breeding bull for slaughter, but failure to do as ordered would bring dire consequences. There went his chances of being able to pay a good bride price in the near future. More urgently, he wondered, "What are they going to do to me? Do they plan to castrate or banish me?"

The day arrived without fanfare. Unmarried young men had gathered logs for a bonfire to be built outside King'oo's kraal. The younger fathers had brought Munyalo's bull and tethered it to a nearby tree.

Sometime after mid-day the older fathers, most of whom were already grandfathers, started gathering. Among them was the young herdsman's father who arrived with several women carrying gourds of the beer he had brewed. The women left as soon as they had carefully placed the gourds on the ground. Of all the fathers, King'oo was the last one to arrive. This signaled the beginning of the ritual; half-gourd bowls of beer began circulating. The bonfire was lit, the bull slaughtered, skinned and cut into pieces for skewering. Eventually they started roasting and eating the meat, making sure they saved the fat.

Clad only in his loincloth, Munyalo squatted near his mother's hut, surrounded by a group of his peers, other single young men from the community who had been circumcised during the same ceremony. Their role was to keep Munyalo from changing his mind, bolting and thus risking banishment. It was a somber gathering, they barely spoke to one another and hardly anyone dared look in the direction where the senior, carousing older fathers sat. Traditionally, this young group was too young to drink alcohol.

The young herdsman was left to stew in his own predicament. He had admitted his responsibility for Kaveke's pregnancy to his father and no one else, but he was sure by now his own mother knew and probably more people in the community, too. He had heard of the *king'ole* but knew very little about its rituals because it took place very rarely and was not a topic that was generally discussed. He was sure there was going to be pain but how he did not know. The old men were letting him sweat it out while they partied and feasted on his bull. The young men patiently waited to be told when to bring Munyalo over to the elders.

More than three hours after they started eating and drinking, there was a pause. Ngumi, the most senior among those gathered, announced through his sharpened teeth that it was time. A circle of sitting elders formed and a signal was flashed to the single young men to bring Munyalo to the tribunal. The young herdsman was left squatting at the center of the circle as the young men departed. They had fulfilled their obligation to the community and their clans and were not allowed to stay to see the punishment.

It was time for the *king'ole* to take over. All was quiet except for the crackling bonfire. All eyes were on Munyalo as he squatted, staring at the ground, his mind refusing to formulate any image of what was about to take place.

"You know why we are here," the grim-visaged, white haired Ngumi bellowed as he glared at him. It was more of a question than a statement. "Then *you* tell us," the pitiless old man demanded.

"I eh, I eh …," squeaked the young man, his voice out of pitch with fear.

"You speak like a woman. Has your randy manhood left you?" Ngumi sneered.

"For all you display as a man you should've screwed the mud in the river," taunted another grim, white haired old man with a Mohawk haircut and several of his front teeth missing.

Munyalo made the mistake of trying to finish what he had started to say which only brought forth further vituperations.

"You show no respect for your elders. You have no respect for anyone," Ngumi thundered. "Speak only when spoken to, you filthy hyena!"

The wrathful outburst made Munyalo cringe in terror and his stomach contracted into a painful knot. Anymore and he would wet himself. He looked around at the gathered group, hoping to find his father's comforting face but did not see him. He was sitting behind and out of sight of his only son, silently watching the drama unfold.

"Is that all you have to say, you depraved seducer of wives? You couldn't have given her any pleasure with *that,*" another old man with heavily stained front teeth mocked, pointing at the young herdsman's crotch.

Suddenly, four of the strongest young fathers seized Munyalo from all sides, pinning him spread eagled on the ground with his face down. Another stripped off the loincloth he was wearing and started smearing his body with the fat from Munyalo's slaughtered bull. When his back and the back of his legs were shiny from the fat the men unceremoniously rolled him over and smeared the front of his body including his genitals.

Munyalo was hoping that this was the final indignity but there was worse to come. The four men, each seizing a limb, picked up and carried the young man face up towards the bonfire. Peering over his side, Munyalo noticed that other elders had been stoking the bonfire. His naked, fat-smeared body was suspended less than a foot from the flames. He fervently wished he could cry out to his father who had always come to his aid in the past but realized he had gone beyond the pale and even his strong father could not help him now.

The circle of elders migrated and reformed around the bonfire. His father stood a few feet beyond his son's head. Late afternoon rain clouds had obscured the sun giving the day an eerie light. Munyalo could see the tips of the flames as sparks rose above them and extinguished themselves in the smoky air above. He was not sure the elders were not going to roast him alive. The heat from the fire was becoming unbearably uncomfortable on the side of his exposed torso and thigh and all he could think of was how to keep from screaming and crying like a baby.

The space above his face darkened and as he focused his eyes he met Ngumi's stern stare. The fierce old man adjusted the blanket draped over his shoulder and gave a slight nod. Munyalo's body tightened as it was swung over the flames. The stench of burnt body hair filled the air. A second nod and the men swung again, this time holding still while flames licked the young man's back and calves. Munyalo let out a grunt as they swung his writhing body away from the punishing flames. He had wet himself from the pain but no one seemed to notice or care. Without a word they turned him over so that his belly faced the ground.

"Are you ready to tell us why we are here?" Ngumi inquired without any note of pity in his voice.

"I did what I shouldn't have done," croaked the terrified young herdsman.

Another old man had squatted next to the young man's face. With his breath reeking of roasted beef, beer and tobacco, he intoned,

"And what was it that you did?"

The burns on his back were beginning to torment him and the thought of more on his stomach and elsewhere prompted Munyalo to answer quickly.

"I took another man's wife."

"You dare call yourself a man with that tiny knob of a prick? You're just a boy not even half-grown," the old man berated him derisively as he slowly got up, straightened his back and nodded to the four strong men. The unexpected swing over the flames made Munyalo let out a pitiful cry as the hair around his genitals was singed. They swung his body off the flames for what was to be the last time but he did not know this.

"Do you swear, on pain of banishment, you'll never do it again?" Ngumi hissed with his lips perilously close to the young man's ear.

"Yes, I swear," the young herdsman nearly screamed.

Without any warning, the four fathers let go and Munyalo flopped unceremoniously on his belly on the rough ground at which he managed to stifle a groan from pain. On a signal all the men turned and left the bonfire site. He lay there still and alone, his mind in a daze, his body hurting and exhausted.

As he silently cursed the inhumane treatment he had

received from the elders, a sudden urge to empty his bowels seized him but instead he vomited the bile he had held back until then. He gazed at the sky worrying about Kaveke, wondering what they had done to her and knowing that he would not be allowed to find out.

The rain that had threatened all day started coming down as he picked himself up to retrieve the cloth he had worn earlier. Each raindrop on his scorched, naked body caused a sharp sting, like a thorn piercing the skin. He staggered towards his refuge, his mother's hut, with the loincloth in his hand

.

FOUR

THE YOUNG PAIR had been punished and penalized but not forgiven. The fear, pain and humiliation left them traumatized and disenchanted with the traditional ways of life. Munyalo's future had turned bleak as his small herd of cattle had no bull to sire the cows and the loss of his herding duties could only lead to a future of poverty. His transgression meant fewer would want him marrying into their families. His father decided to move his homestead away from King'oo's kraal and thus shield his son from further temptation as well as spare the family any incidental and additional embarrassment.

As if a curse had been cast upon the young man, less than a year after his father moved the family, Munyalo's herd was decimated by a rinderpest epidemic that left him with only two young and scrawny heifers. After this blow to his wealth he decided to leave the homestead and look for better prospects beyond the tribal boundaries. He traveled to the port town of Mombasa where he found employment as a porter with the East African Railways and Harbours. Fortunately for him, the railway system was expanding and that made it easier for him to gain employment.

Non-tribal ideas did not take long to engage the lonely Munyalo. He had kept to himself, wary of worldly town-folk, until a fellow porter introduced him to the Christian religion. This, he felt, was safe as the church discouraged sex among its young, unmarried members. He had been caught once and Munyalo did not care to repeat the experience. Besides, even though he had sworn off Kaveke, he often thought of his first love.

In the meantime, Kaveke's life was just as traumatic. The first wife, jealous of her youth and angry about her betrayal, used the young wife's misdeed as an extra lever to extract more labor out of the poor young woman. "Mother" no longer displayed any feeling of affection towards the youngest wife. When her pregnancy slowed her down, the first wife berated her for being lazy.

"You're just as worthless as you are thoughtless," "Mother" would accuse her. "I should send you back to your family. You're of no use to me."

Even though the first wife was truly a mother to her own children, she was unwilling to forgive the youngest wife for bringing shame to the leading family in the community. The older woman's vindictiveness and malice continued to torment Kaveke until she became so overwrought that in the end she miscarried.

Throughout the ordeal Kaveke suffered in silence.

Less than a year after the loss of her child, their infirm husband was accidentally trampled to death by his own herd of cattle. First wife's son, as the new head of the family, decided to send Kaveke back to her parents' homestead because his mother was always complaining about her. Anyone interested in marrying her would then be expected to pay back the bride price given to her parents by King'oo. That diminished her chances of her ever finding a husband of about the right age but she did not care. She had been married off once and did not relish the idea of being given to another old man with senior wives. She had to find a way to break out of that cycle, she just did not know how.

Kaveke's parents were anxious to get their "damaged" daughter married off and thus remove their obligation to King'oo's family. As they ticked off the years they became less hopeful because their daughter was getting too old for marriage. On her twenty-first birthday they gave up. That same year, a man came to the village to talk about a new set of beliefs about the world that taught forgiveness and forbade the paying of bride price for wives. He was the first Christian preacher sent out to evangelize the people of Kithongoto.

One day Kaveke's mother, in desperation, suggested, "May be you should go and hear this man."

"Why should I? Is he going to give me a husband I like?"

"As if you're in any position to choose. Staying here has not helped, has it? Besides, I did not see a woman accompanying him."

"Mother! He's so old he's got one foot in the grave."

Her mother shrugged her shoulders dismissively, a sign that she had nothing more to say.

The following Sunday Kaveke went to hear the preacher. She did not understand most of what the old man said but found his voice soothing. She did however notice there were other people of about her age, people she had not met before. A man half the preacher's age introduced himself.

"I'm David. This must be your first time here."

"How would you know that?"

"I help the pastor set up every Sunday and meet everyone who comes to hear him. What's your name?" David asked.

"Kaveke," she answered shyly.

"Did you like the sermon?"

"The what?"

"The preacher's words," he clarified.

"I didn't understand most of it but I liked his voice."

"Well, if you would like to understand more, come to our early Sunday morning meetings. We meet every week, before the general service to discuss how one should live according to the Bible. The Bible is the book where these beliefs are written down and some of us are learning to read and write, too."

"I'll think about it," Kaveke said as she turned away. She was getting self-conscious about the attention the young man seemed to show. She was not sure he was not flirting with her. She did not like him that much, so she skipped the next Sunday even though she wanted to know more about this religion called Christianity. Nonetheless, that first sermon marked the beginning of Kaveke's conversion. By the time Pastor e'Muthembwa came to take over from the succession of preachers and energize the failing church she was deeply involved in winning souls for Christ.

She was satisfied with her work in the church but Kaveke remained unfulfilled; she was approaching twenty-three years of age and still unmarried. She had seen five pastors come and go, some in disgrace. She was not sure what type of preacher the latest one was. He stirred in her a mixture of awe, admiration and the type of sensual desire she had known briefly many years ago. Was it true that all good Christian pastors could have one wife only? She decided to get close to the new pastor through hard work and kindness.

"Maybe he is not married," she thought.

It was during the fifth month after his arrival in Kithongoto that e'Muthembwa had a crisis of conscience and reached a turning point in his missionary work. An attractive, widowed female congregant, who had been very active in the church and helpful in organizing other women to make sure the preacher always had water in his house, decided while e'Muthembwa was away from his house she was going to prepare his supper. As he approached he encountered delicious aromas wafting from his house. For a brief moment he thought his wife had decided to surprise him. Surely she could not have left all the children home just to visit him. He thought the pressure, the heat and the loneliness were beginning to affect his perception of what was real. He stood still and took a deep breath to clear his mind, while his mouth watered.

He slowly walked up to the open door and peered inside. Kaveke had not heard him approach. As his shadow darkened the doorway she gave a cry, a mixture of fright and joy.

"Oh, pastor! You caught me. I did not hear you come up," she cooed.

"What are you doing here? I thought I made it clear that I did not want anyone entering my house in my absence.

Why did you not leave the water under the eaves as we agreed?" he demanded as he stood just outside the door. He realized his tone was unintentionally harsh. He actually liked the woman and was grateful for her help but he did not trust himself with her in his house.

"You can at least thank me for cooking your supper. I'll dish it up for you. Come! Sit down and eat. When is the last time you had a home cooked meal in your own house?"

"Thank you. I've already had my supper," he fibbed. "Just leave the food in the pot. I'll take care of it later," e'Muthembwa said in a kinder tone but without any intention of entering the house as long as she was there.

The attractive widow just sat and stared at him, her eyes daring him to approach her. Yes, the flesh was all too willing but his faith said otherwise. He steeled himself and stayed put. In a ministerial voice, e'Muthembwa intoned,

"Let us bow our heads in prayer." And without waiting he launched into Psalm 23: 'The Lord is my shepherd; I shall not want…' By the time he had got to dwelling 'in the house of the Lord forever' followed by 'Amen' he was ready to send the woman packing. He stepped to one side of the door and as kindly as he could said to her,

"Thank you again, sister. Now leave and may the Lord guide you."

She calmly got up, gathered herself and left without saying a single word. She did not know what to make of this man of God but she was sure that over time she would find out.

That night e'Muthembwa prayed hard for the Lord to give him the strength to persevere but in the end he concluded that abstinence was not a wise and safe way of life. Was the Lord telling him to go get his wife? The following day he decided it was time he brought his wife and children to live with him. It was early in the week and without letting anyone know what he was up to, he got on his bicycle and peddled the forty or so miles to the railway station. Late afternoon the following day he was home with his family.

The water providers thought he was rejecting their help when no one moved the water gourds left under the eaves of his house. Soon enough everyone realized e'Muthembwa was no longer living there. For several days, it was said even the proud preacher could not hack it and like a thief had evaporated into thin air under the cover of darkness. The tongue waggers were dumbfounded when he showed up the following Saturday with a brood of children and a wife in tow. They could not believe what they were seeing.

What they did not know was that more than ever before he was determined to show them that not all preachers were hypocrites. He was sure he could nurture that congregation until they became true believers. In fact, while away he had contacted the missionaries who sponsored his church and told them to stop looking for a replacement for him, that he had found the parish where he wanted to spend the rest of his days preaching. He was moving his family permanently to the parish he was serving. Although this was a shock to them, they knew better than to suggest anything different because e'Muthembwa was notorious for being stubborn. Besides, there was no one else willing to go and minister to the congregation at Kithongoto, so they acquiesced.

With his wife and children living with him some of the pressure was now lifted and he could concentrate on expanding the congregation. He set out to establish permanent friendships by fully sharing his expertise in farming and building. He bought a hand plough and four untrained oxen,

fashioned wooden yokes and leather straps for keeping the
yokes on the beasts and then trained the oxen. By the next
planting season e'Muthembwa had expanded his cultivated
fields to nearly eleven acres. In the process, he enlisted the
help of several members of the congregation.

Everything was evolving just the way he had imagined
it. Some were curious about this industrious newcomer.
Others were ready to learn and copy his new farming methods while learning about the scriptures. Unfortunately, some
of these new converts understood the quality of 'meek and
mild' to be a virtue of the preacher that did not apply to
them. They thought it meant they could take advantage of
him and he would turn the other cheek; however, they found
out that such was not the preacher's temperament.

Musyoka, a happy-go-lucky young man employed in the
community, decided to hijack e'Muthembwa's bicycle from
the preacher's thirteen year-old son. Mutunga, the youngster,
had been entrusted with his father's only means of transportation to enable him to carry a four-gallon container of
water from the well for the daily household supply.

While the boy was filling up the container, Musyoka got
on the bicycle and told the youth that he was going to ride it
around for a few minutes but when the boy turned to load the
water on the bicycle, Musyoka was gone and the bicycle with
him. When he did not return by nightfall, the preacher's son
went home dejected and without any water, fearfully walking
the entire mile and a half distance in the darkness of night.
He was afraid of his father's reaction as well as the wild
animals he might come across. He knew he had let the family
down.

After Mutunga nervously explained to his father what
had happened, the preacher said nothing but his wife sensed

he was seething, a volcano ready to erupt. With inadequate water for cooking, the family went without supper that night. The following day, e'Muthembwa had no means of getting to the house of a sick member of the church and was therefore unable to fulfill one of the major responsibilities of a preacher, to minister to his flock. He also could not keep an appointment with the local chief, a crucial meeting during which they were going to discuss the acquisition of land for an elementary school he hoped to help start.

The audacious and inconsiderate youth did not return with the bicycle from a clandestine visit to his girlfriend's home until late afternoon the next day. As he happily pedaled the bicycle to the preacher's home he met a murderous looking e'Muthembwa, barely out of his own house, on his way to the young man's home.

"Good afternoon pastor," Musyoka called out cheerfully.

"Stop! Musyoka! *Tutagombana,*"[1] the preacher roared, relapsing into the lingua franca of Kiswahili. The errant young man almost fell off the bicycle from shock as he dismounted suddenly. He was barely two feet away from the preacher who he noticed was absolutely livid. It was not until that moment that the presumptuous young man noticed the long walking stick e'Muthembwa was carrying. The preacher moved in even closer, locked eyes with Musyoka and demanded,

"How dare you take my bicycle without permission? Do you think all I have to do is wait around for you to return at your convenience? I'm going to teach you a lesson you should have learnt when you were a little boy. You're big

---

[1] We've a quarrel to settle

enough to take something from a small child. Let's see how
you do when you tangle with a man. Put the bicycle down.
You and I have some business to settle."

As the last word left his lips, e'Muthembwa raised the
staff. Musyoka saw it coming down, ducked and in the same
movement, grabbed the bicycle, jumped on and pedaled out
of there as fast as his legs would go. The staff cut a whoosh-
ing arc through the air and struck the ground with a dull
thud.

Throughout the encounter Kanini, who had come out of
their house when she heard her husband's angry voice, stood
several paces behind him. As the young man raced away, she
walked up to her husband and asked quietly,

"Were you really going to beat him up? Imagine what it
would have done to your ministry."

E'Muthembwa, with the sudden spike of adrenaline still
coursing through his body, made a derisive grunt and as he
turned to walk back to the house declared,

"I'm not ready to suffer impudent fools."

When he entered the house, he brusquely grabbed a
chair, carried it outside and plunked it down under the eaves,
a few paces from the door. Still fuming, he leaned on his big
stick as he sat down and glared into space. A little while later
his wife brought him a cup of tea and no more was said about
Musyoka and the bicycle. In his prayers that night he asked
the good Lord to grant him the fortitude to suffer the inconsiderate and conquer his temper.

The day after the near altercation and without offering
any apology, an emissary from Musyoka delivered the bicycle and within a week the inconsiderate and arrogant young
man moved away from the community.

FIVE

THE CONGREGATION CONTINUED to grow even though many elders were antagonistic to the new religion; more and more people were joining the church every month and attending catechism to learn the tenets of Christianity. Some of the young people were doing so without their families' blessings. E'Muthembwa's dream of husbanding a thriving church was coming to fruition and every night he thanked the Lord for allowing him to harvest souls for Christ. What he did not imagine was the mysterious ways in which such a gathering could make the unexpected happen.

He decided it was time to construct a larger building, a more permanent structure, as a sign to the community that the church was there to stay. He chose to site the new building a few meters from a nearby prominent baobab tree, a symbolism which did not go unnoticed by the community. The seemingly upside down but majestic baobab tree and its gourd-shaped fruit is admired for its resiliency in growing over many years into an enormous size in the face of perennial water shortage and constant de-barking by people for rope material or medicine. It survives deep wounds caused by stakes driven into its trunk by the locals climbing up to hang their beehives or attacks by elephants looking for both moisture and fiber. Higher branches that are not ripped off in these assaults grow to produce pods full of edible pulp which tides people over during periods of food shortage. It is indeed the tree of life that all adversity leaves unscathed and still growing.

His skills came into use as he organized the congregation into a building committee, parceling out responsibilities according to each person's abilities. The result was a corrugated iron roof, steel-frame glass-windows, cinderblock building with a brown-stained concrete floor. Few in the neighborhood had been inside such a modern building before. It was no surprise that there were several new faces in the crowd that came to celebrate the first Sunday service in the new church.

Concurrently, he started a bible study class at the local elementary school, which he had helped build. Throughout these new developments, widow Kaveke continued to play a major part in the church activities: she volunteered to help Kanini settle in and introduced her to other female members of the congregation. By then, she was acting as if she were a younger sister of the preacher's wife. She had found a new respect for e'Muthembwa.

Almost a year and a half after the preacher's family joined him at Kithongoto, a man in his early thirties came to the Sunday church service. The usual two-person welcome committee greeted him. His appearance was that of a man from an urban area. He had on shiny brown leather shoes, a white shirt with tie and light brown slacks with a checkered matching wool jacket. No one recognized the young man who introduced himself as Daniel even though he was in fact a local boy returned home. Through his contacts with missionaries at the coast Munyalo had learnt to read, write and understand simple English phrases. His baptismal name was Daniel. He had moved up in his employment and done well. Now he was returning to his ancestral area with the intention of buying land where he could build a house away from town life.

As was the pastor's custom, he stood at the church door at the end of the service, greeting and thanking all those who had come to hear the Word.

"We're glad you joined us today," pastor e'Muthembwa said as he shook the young man's hand.

"It was a wonderful sermon. I'm looking forward to next week," Daniel responded.

"I haven't seen you before. Do you have family around here?" the pastor asked.

"I was born near King'oo's home but my father moved to Matuu village. I'm on leave for three weeks from my work in Mombasa."

"I welcome you again to our church," said the pastor as he shifted his attention to greet the next congregant.

At that moment Kaveke, as usual, was coming out of the building with e'Muthembwa's wife and children. She took a deep breath but could not seem to get enough air. Could it be Munyalo talking to the pastor? It had been so many years that she could not be sure but she was almost certain it was his voice. She had to overcome her public shyness towards men and confront the stranger. Hurriedly she walked past the pastor and called out,

"Munyalo!"

The young man froze mid-step as if he was doing a pantomime. He had walked no more than a few yards away from the pastor. Kaveke caught up with him, heart pounding, afraid it might turn out to be all a dream. She had never stopped caring for him.

Daniel turned eagerly to face her, uncertain as to who had called out his name. He was speechless when he recognized the face of his long lost love, now slightly marked with age but mature, more confident and still beautiful. All those years he lived at the coast he never fell in love with anyone else. His father had made him promise, on pain of being disowned, that he would never go near "that woman." He didn't know what had happened to her since then but was taken so by surprise that he didn't have time to consult his conscience but stammered a one-word question,

"K-kaveke?"

If it had been appropriate to embrace they would have but such an act would have been scandalous at church. Instead, they stood there, inspecting each other.

"Look at you. All dressed up like town people," she chided gently. "Where did you come from?"

"Mombasa. You probably heard me tell the pastor I'm on leave."

"On leave from what? What's it you do at the coast?"

"It's a long story."

They had so many questions to ask each other, so many years to fill in, that neither seemed to have the patience to wait for the other to answer. Besides, several of the churchgoers had stopped to watch this new interaction. Finally Daniel found his voice and quietly asked,

"Can we get together and talk without getting into

56

trouble?"

"I would love to. This time the only trouble will be from me," she said softly, and gave him an almost imperceptible wink. Daniel realized his heart was racing like that of a teenager. Reading mischief in Kaveke's eyes, he smiled and added,

"I can hardly wait."

The shrewd preacher made a mental note of the whole exchange. Rather than have one of his staunch congregants going astray by surreptitiously meeting the new young man he asked his wife to invite Kaveke and Daniel for tea. The occasion would give them the opportunity to be reacquainted without causing a scandal. It would also offer the preacher the chance to interview the new young stranger. It was obvious to him that sometime in their past they had cared for each other.

So, during tea the preacher asked Daniel about his family and the kind of work he did as well as the type of church the young man attended at the coast. Afterwards, e'Muthembwa suggested the young pair go out and sit in the shade of a nearby tree and get re-acquainted, indeed a chaperoned outing.

They talked for almost five hours, always conscious that the preacher was not too far away. They would have continued if darkness had not intervened. Munyalo had learnt by then that Kaveke was widowed and he no longer had to feel guilty about seeing her.

By the third Sunday they had fully re-kindled their long dormant love and announced that they wanted e'Muthembwa to officiate at their wedding. He never had the opportunity to perform this solemn ritual for anyone in all the churches he had preached. Pastor e'Muthembwa looked forward to finally marrying one of his flock in the Christian way and he could think of no one more deserving of the honor of being the first Christian married woman in the village. Kaveke had been the glue that held the women in the church together.

Imagine his disbelief and frustration when he went to the mission head office to collect the appropriate forms only to be informed that he needed additional training if he was going to officiate at any marriage ceremony. The missionaries who had trained him had not told him that he was not qualified to perform such a function; the occasion never arose since no couples at Kithongoto had wanted to renew their traditional pledges in a Christian ceremony. For the sake of Daniel Munyalo and Kaveke he swallowed his anger and calmly arranged for a white missionary to come to Kithongoto to officiate at their wedding. As a consolation, he was asked to help in leading the ceremony.

In the years following Daniel and Kaveke's marriage and unaware that it would put him at odds with the white missionaries, e'Muthembwa successfully completed more training at the seminary in Mumbuni to qualify him to officiate at marriage ceremonies, a function that had been hitherto the exclusive domain of the white foreigners. Even though he was now referred to as Reverend Gideon e'Muthembwa, the politics of the white missionary church precluded him from performing all the functions for which he had been trained.

After agitating for a year for status befitting his level of training and experience, he and other like-minded African preachers mutinied and left their original denomination to establish a new African-based church. The rituals of the new denomination were very similar to those of the preacher's former church. To set themselves apart, ordained ministers in the new church decided to wear clerical collars, which the minister's former church considered a worldly adornment.

His congregation became very distressed when they got wind of his intention to move his family and start a new church elsewhere under the new rules. They formed a delegation and went to plead with the preacher to stay but they were unable to persuade him to remain in this church with unequal rights. He would not budge. To keep him at Kithongoto, the church leaders negotiated with the original denomination and bought the church property. In essence, the unyielding preacher had hijacked the congregation at Kithongoto. He could now rightfully and legally officiate at marriage ceremonies in his own church and collect the small stipend that was regularly offered for this service.

He was disappointed and disillusioned that he had to leave his original church to get the same rights as the white preachers, but the change fired up this earnest man of God; he busied himself with strengthening the congregation. Several men had shown interest in being trained as pastors and e'Muthembwa was all too eager to get them into Bible School at Kangundo, where he had been trained.

It made no difference that Timothy Muthengi, his barely literate friend and the first to be admitted to the school, ended up joining the pastor's original denomination. That the eager deacon, though not the brightest of individuals, was going into the ministry made the reverend proud; his evangelical work was bearing fruit beyond his expectations.

Timothy was one of the few close friends Reverend e'Muthembwa had at Kithongoto. When the two were not planning some church function they often sat in the shade of the tree next to the preacher's outdoor carpentry shop to tell stories from the "old days." The funnier the better. One slow afternoon the preacher offered the following story about a simpleton who had never been out of his village:

> *Kiangi was born three years after the Mombasa – Kisumu railway came through the arid savannah plains of his homeland. Few among his people had traveled beyond the tribal borders and even fewer knew anything about mechanized transportation. In fact, their contacts with the outside world had been limited to cattle raiding excursions into the neighboring Maasai lands so it was no wonder that everyone talked with awe about the arrival of the behemoth millipede that belched smoke as it ran angrily up and down the western tribal plains.*
>
> *On his eighteenth birthday, Kiangi decided he was going to learn more about the millipede, something that had fascinated him throughout his young life. One morning he wrapped a small lump of mashed maize and beans in boiled banana leaves and set out on foot. He walked the fifty or so miles between his rural homestead and Nairobi, the largest town in the country at the time, to present himself for employment as a signal trainee at the Muthurwa Railway Training School.*
>
> *Although the colonial government was keen to hire many Africans to manage the several train stations along the line, few of the locals wanted anything to do with the angry millipede. It was something they feared and therefore shunned. An eager recruit for training was indeed welcome, even though the illiterate Kiangi barely understood Chaundry, his Indian instructor. Neither Chaundry*

nor Kiangi was proficient in Kiswahili, the local lingua franca in which training was to be conducted.

A week of oral instructions in the corrugated-iron roof shed that served as his classroom did nothing to lessen Kiangi's ignorance of train signaling. Now his training moved out to the railway marshalling yard. For that part of his instructions he was given three colored flags: red, yellow and green. Each was mounted on a short staff.

It was not long before Kiangi, with his flags, was sent out into the railway marshalling yard. He immediately noticed the millipedes had been cut up into pieces. Now each headpiece was snorting louder than he had ever heard. He watched as a more experienced trainee waved flags identical to those Kiangi had been given, to direct different engineers who moved the train engines to pick up various carriages. Kiangi considered the gigantic millipede heads to have the temper of a randy bull that had been kept away from the heifers for too long.

He observed that waving the red flag made the noisy behemoths stop, the yellow made them move slowly. He thought that when the green was waved the monsters ignored the flag and took off at high speed but that none of the flags seemed to appease their anger. The ochre-red and wasp-yellow contraptions were like bulls – always snorting especially when they faced one another. He knew nothing about the mechanics of pneumatic brakes.

Shortly it was his turn to wave the flags, to orchestrate what he figured was a purposeless movement of the giants. Soon Kiangi had two "bulls" facing each other, glaring and snorting. A third one passed close by but seemed completely unconcerned about the two squaring off. His gaze returned to the two combatants still spewing "smoke."

'Let them fight it out. May be they'll then be quiet enough for me to concentrate,' he thought. He could not bear their standing there, simply taunting each other. He waved the yellow flag at one and then the other. Nothing happened! He waved in the opposite direction, this time using the green flag. That seemed to assuage their fury as each backed away. When they were about fifty yards apart they stopped, snorted and let out a deafening hiss.

'Now I know they are pissed off. I'll let them settle it once for all before I go deaf,' Kiangi decided. He waved the yellow flag at each beast, thus urging them forward until their front bumpers hit. The ensuing crash made the instructor run outside into the marshalling yard.

"What in the name of all that is unholy are you doing?" Chaundry demanded.

"Aeeeh! They have been taunting each other all morning. I got tired and let them fight it out. Maybe they will now be quiet while I work," Kiangi replied in a garbled mixture of his native tongue and Kiswahili.

"What are you talking about? Surely you can't be serious," retorted the exasperated instructor.

"Can't you hear them? They are still angry," he replied, incredulous that Chaundry was so hard of hearing.

If there had been many applicants willing to work for the railway Kiangi would have been fired on the spot; however, luck was on his side for Chaundry realized Kiangi had failed to understand any of the oral instructions.

"Come here!" he commanded. When Kiangi came over the Indian instructor grabbed the flags. He held up the red flag.

"When you wave this it tells the engineer to stop. You must make sure he sees it," Chaundry instructed.

"What's an engineer? Who is supposed to see the flag? There's no one here but these angry behemoths," Kiangi countered.

"Look up there," Chaundry pointed impatiently at one of the engines.

Totally flustered Kiangi reverted to his mother tongue, "All I see is the angry bull."

Gazing on the bewildered angry face it dawned on Chaundry that Kiangi had understood nothing. He started walking towards one of the stationary engines.

"Come with me," he said as he motioned to Kiangi. The young villager, careful to make sure he kept the instructor between himself and the snorting bull in case it charged, followed the Indian.

"Mr. Singh," Chaundry called out as he approached the train engine. "Please come down for a minute."

The Sikh engineer opened a side door and grabbed the handle to climb down. Having never seen a man whose normal head was bandaged Kiangi was sure the small man with dark grease-smudges on his uniform had been injured by the angry bull and the huge thing was now sizing up its next victim. He stood still ready to flee. However, before Kiangi could make his escape his instructor pointed at the turbaned man,

"This is Mr. Singh, the engineer of this train. Each train has an engineer."

Kiangi was puzzled; he did not make the connection between the behemoth's movements and the small man with the bandaged head. Besides, he was only guessing at what his instructor had said. The man seemed uninjured and therefore had to have powerful witchcraft to have survived the snorting, smoke-belching demon. At that point Chaundry spoke in a tongue which Kiangi did not recognize and the engineer climbed back into the engine cabin.

"Now," Chaundry said, turning towards Kiangi, 'This flag (holding up the yellow) tells the engineer to move the train slowly. Move it from left to right if you want him to go right or right to left if you want him to go left. Do you follow?" Kiangi remained wide-eyed and puzzled.

"Angalia," (Watch) the instructor said in Kiswahili, as he waved the yellow flag at Mr. Singh to move in one direction and then the other.

"Ndio bwana." (Yes, sir) answered Kiangi respectfully in the same language.

"Waving this flag," Chaundry explained as best he could in Kiswahili, holding the green color, *"tells the engineer he may go as fast as he can safely go in the direction you indicate."* The instructor waved the green flag at another engineer whose train was ready to pull out of the marshalling yard.

"Aaah!" was Kiangi's reaction, apparently enlightened.

"This," said the Indian as he held up the red flag *"tells the engineer to stop."* The instructor waved it at another oncoming engine and it stopped.

Kiangi's understanding went only as far the meaning of the flags. He understood little about the shunting of the trains or the fact that they traveled only on the rails. In essence, he just didn't get it; how the whole system worked was totally beyond his rural imagination. He never mastered the art of train traffic signaling and in the end he gained employment as a manual laborer, to work in repairing the rail line in the section along his tribal homeland. He was a happy man!

Six

WHEN THE NEW building was opened the church did not have enough money for a bell. An old two-foot long rail piece discarded from the building of the Mombasa-Nairobi railway, hung by wire on a tree outside the building, continued to summon the faithful every Sunday. The bell ringer used an old, disfigured, foot-long metal bolt to whack the suspended rail, changing the rhythm according to how soon the service was going to start. About a minute long pause between gongs meant you had plenty of time to get there but a fast staccato told the congregants the service was about to begin.

Clocks and watches were rare around Kithongoto, a convenient situation which allowed the preacher to time the service according to how much he had to say each Sunday. It could be anywhere between one to two and a half hours long. The absence of timepieces was of little consequence since the people used the sun to time their daily activities. In this equatorial country it rose and set at about the same time each day throughout the year, six in the morning and six in the evening.

Stories were the main entertainment and an integral part of life in this culture where daylight lasted only twelve hours a day and the only light after dark was a fire in the kitchen hut where the family gathered for the evening meal. The reverend often told stories as a way to drive home a moral point. In fact, he would use a story as the basis for his Sunday sermon. One Sunday the topic was God's constant hand in our daily lives. The sermon was titled *God's Promise*. He began by dramatically telling the following story:

"It was the end of the dry season. The wisps of dust and soft winds had decreased considerably. That night, as the sun went down the light wind that had been blowing all day stopped. It became eerily quiet and the earlier clear skies turned dark. The air smelt of moisture as they sat down for their late supper. It was so quiet one could hear an ant walking.

"Mwengi's family had supper in the darkened kitchen as was the custom, embers from the dying cooking fire provided the only light there was. It was a good thing they used their fingers to pick out morsels of food from the half gourds they used for plates because they would otherwise not have been able to see their plates. All Mwengi could hear was chewing as his brothers and sisters made their way through the pile of maize and beans in their shared half gourd.

"*Suddenly* there was a faint glimmer of light, as if someone with a weak bicycle battery had quietly whizzed past the door of their windowless mud-hut kitchen. No one said anything. Moments later, another light display, this time much brighter, flickered past the kitchen door. Just as quickly, they were back to darkness and the sound of chewing. He knew it was going to rain but when, Mwengi did not know.

"Then a few loud and heavy rain drops thudded on the ground outside and nothing more. Five or so minutes later everything was instantly illuminated as if daylight had arrived. Almost instantaneously the thunder started. First, it sounded as if someone was running a stick on a dry, wrinkled cowhide. Then the deafening series of booms: kraaack, kraack, BOOM, BOOM, BOom.

"The first boom found his older brother crouching in the farthest point away from the door. For him, this was frightening, but Mwengi was excited; he looked forward to the next big boom and he was not disappointed. It occurred as the rain began to come down heavily. There was no wind, just big drops of rain, accompanied by thunder and lightning. The dance drums had reached their crescendo.

After a while he began to wonder whether it was going to let up to allow the family to scurry from the kitchen hut to the main building where they slept. Mwengi did not relish the thought of having to go to bed in wet clothes. They slept in their day clothes since there was no extra money for the luxury of buying pajamas. There was hardly enough to meet the large family's basic needs.

"Miracle of miracles, just as they finished their supper there was a lull in the downpour, long enough for the family to hurry to their beds.

"That night's downpour marked the beginning of the long rainy season. During the previous season, the rains had failed and the crops had withered in the fields without maturing, so the rations had been meager for almost five months. His parents had been anxiously waiting for this welcome deluge. For the young ones it meant there would be plenty to eat as the year progressed.

"Early the following day his mother was all excited. It was time to sow millet in the fields and she with the older children went out into their field that day while Mwengi stayed home to watch over his younger sisters. But, he was worried because he knew that the last time his parents planted millet his older brothers and sisters had been woken up before dawn to go into the field to frighten away the weaverbirds from the millet as it matured on the stalks and now he was old enough to be given this chore. Mwengi found some consolation in that the day he would be sent out into the field was still several weeks in the future.

"Within a week the clumps of millet stalks were coming up. His parents and older siblings, when they were not in school or herding the family cattle and goats, were out weeding around the growing millet. Less than two months later, the first heads were evident on the taller stalks. In less than two weeks after that, the field was covered with millet stalks, each terminating in a banana-size head full of maturing millet grains.

"Members of Mwengi's family were not the only creatures monitoring this change: the weaver birds were ready to pick the first crop. It was a case of whoever got to it first got to keep it. Therefore it was incumbent upon the humans to keep the pests from their ripening food. His mother would wake up one of the older siblings before dawn and send the child to guard the millet grains. Knowing that the family never had its meals early enough for one to go to bed and get enough rest before dawn, Mwengi dreaded the day he would be asked to go shoo the birds away. He was sure this was the season he would have to start guarding the millet.

"His day arrived two weeks into the guarding stint. The morning his mother woke him up he stumbled out of bed and headed for the field. Dawn was just breaking; he could still see the morning star in the sky as he picked his way along the short stony path that led to the verdant millet field. About three hours later his mother, carrying his baby sister on her back, joined him. She put the sleepy baby next to a clump of millet stalks and asked him to watch over her while his mother went to weed a patch of the field a short distance away as well as look out for the odd weaver bird straggler.

"Mwengi welcomed the change of duty since he did not have to keep his eyes peeled constantly for the marauding birds. Most of them made their raids at daybreak and by early mid-morning they would return to their nests where they would remain until the late afternoon. He knew all he had to do was to listen for his sister's whimpering. So, in the warm and humid field, he sat under the nearest shade and dozed on and off.

"He had no idea how long his eyes had been closed. Less than five feet away the baby was now sitting up, giggling and playing with something. As his eyes focused he recognized the toy she was trying to pin down, a full-grown cobra! His baby sister was completely absorbed in subduing her shiny brown and white toy.

"The cobra was halfway coiled around one of the baby's chubby legs, its head level with his sister's face. She in turn was trying to grab the swaying head but the cobra wanted to get away. Every time the snake freed enough of its body to sway its head, a little hand would reach out for its neck and with great glee seize it. Any movement by either made him sick to his stomach with fear and foreboding. What could he do? Mwengi realized that any sudden movement on his part might frighten the snake and make it strike. He watched despairingly wondering how he could rescue her. 'God, please don't let it bite my sister,' he prayed urgently.

"All of a sudden the snake seemed to tire of moving its head from side to side and his baby sister lost interest and stopped reaching for it. That was the chance the cobra had waited for and it quickly slithered into the nearest clump of millet stalks. In a split second Mwengi jumped and scooped up his sister, leaving her bedding where it had been and ran towards where he thought their mother was.

"'Why are you bringing the baby now?' his mother demanded. 'I didn't hear her cry.'

"Mwengi's mouth was too dry with fright to respond immediately.

"'Now that you've woken her up you'll have to carry her around while I finish weeding this patch. Go get the baby basket.'

"Off he went to get the leather harness that he used for carrying his sister on his back. As he walked back to where the baby had been sleeping Mwengi was sure the cobra had not gone very far. He quickly picked up the harness, shook it for good measure and hurried back to where his mother was waiting. In the meantime, he decided not to mention the snake in case his mother scolded him for not staying awake."

E'Muthembwa took a long, pensive pause then asked the congregation,

"Why didn't the serpent strike?" Another poignant pause followed.

"As it's written in Psalm 121 verses 5 and 7 the Lord is our keeper and will keep all evil from us, if we believe in Him. 'For the eyes of the Lord *are* over the righteous, and his ears *are open* unto their prayers: but the face of the Lord *is* against them that do evil.' That is God's promise as declared in 1 Peter 3:12. Let us bow our heads in prayer."

Within a few years and unlike the slow-growing baobab tree, church membership grew considerably. It was time to build a proper church. The reverend convened a building committee to find and hire a builder for a modern building. He was amazed by the enthusiasm with which the congregation picked up the idea.

With little outside financial help they were able to raise a stone and brick building, siting it higher on the same ridge as the original church of mud and thatch. A tile roof kept the entire building cool on hot days. One of the transepts was the church office and the other a large multipurpose room. Light from the tall glass windows gave the new wooden benches in the nave a warm, intimate hue, and the roof over the east-facing apse supported a brown steeple inside which a triple-tone church bell was installed. The outside of the steeple was topped with a white, metal cross with an attached grounding wire. A raised floor inside the church apse supported a varnished wooden pulpit with a single microphone. Final touches included a battery-powered PA system and several floodlights with a diesel electric generator for lighting evening services.

There were almost four hundred regular members when the church opened its own grades one-through-eight school. Several members from the late King'oo's family had converted to Christianity and two of his sons were now active in the church. Reverend e'Muthembwa constituted various committees to help run some of the church functions such as outreach, education, family well-being or counseling, among others. As a lover of music with a beautiful pitch-perfect voice, he took upon himself the responsibility of starting an *a cappella* church choir whose members were mainly the youth in the congregation. His son and daughter, Joseph Mutunga and Esther Ndoti, were members of the choir as well as leaders in Sunday school until they qualified for admission to boarding high schools, far away from home.

That his own children were in school gave the preacher a degree of believability when he stressed the importance of education in the community. Through his efforts several children of his initial converts were now receiving college education as well as professional training. Among these was Priscilla Katee, a petite young woman, who was studying for a career in rural nutrition. She was the oldest daughter of one of the church deacons. In a few more years going on to higher education would be the norm but Priscilla, the preacher's two children and a few others were the 'miracle babies', the first wave from Kithongoto elementary school to earn a place in post-high school institutions, the first to complete a college program culminating in a degree.

E'Muthembwa strongly believed in the value of formal education but did not fully comprehend the consequences of such an undertaking. All he had ever had was the equivalent of fourth grade schooling. As the result of such limited education he was often surprised by what his own children were learning at school. The belief in a round earth was beyond his comprehension and that all the different people on earth shared the same sun remained a mystery to him. He had not anticipated that education would change the young generation's traditional outlook, that it would make one think in global terms rather than the limited tribal outlook.

As the indigent preacher encouraged them to aim high, his son and daughter fortunately did well enough in school to merit various types of scholarships. When Mutunga and Ndoti qualified for post high-school education and training their father was disappointed that he could give them no advice on what careers they should pursue. They were on their own. What was certain was that their father was sure he wanted them to have better lives than he had.

The preacher could not share in his children's new experiences in "the white" world. Indeed, with 'this education business' the old world was changing, every year there were aspects of Mutunga's and Ndoti's lives which e'Muthembwa could not comprehend or appreciate. Traditionally, daughters did not talk back to their fathers and sons did not challenge their parents' version of the truth. Now both children dared express their opinions on matters pertaining to their own lives.

Hence, the preacher was not surprised when his son, after his graduation from university, was employed somewhere in Nairobi. He said nothing even though he was disturbed by his son's decision to live so far away. To the children, it seemed the preacher did not even notice they no longer attended church regularly.

During one of his visits with his parents a year after Mutunga started working he was taken off guard when his mother brought up the subject of marriage. Like all mothers of her era, she was anxious to see her son through the final stage of his progression into full adulthood, a final passage that was marked by marriage and the raising of one's family. According to tradition, she expected her son to name the girl he had chosen to be his wife, after which she and the reverend would start negotiations with their son's future in-laws, if they approved of the girl's family. Mutunga had often wondered unsuccessfully how he could make his parents realize the old ways were no longer applicable to his marriage plans, that for his generation all one needed was to court the woman and if she was amenable to marriage then both sets of parents would be invited to the ceremony.

"Now that you've finished your education you should be thinking of getting a wife," said his mother.

"I am, mother," he said nervously.

She thought her son was acting strangely but continued as if she hadn't noticed anything, "Have you already found the girl? Your father and I will be all too happy to go and negotiate with her family."

"I don't think that will be necessary."

"What? Everyone comes from a family," she remarked. This was true in a society where uncles and aunts took over as parents for children whose fathers and mothers had died unexpectedly.

"I know that! The person I'm thinking of marrying may not need her parents to negotiate with either you or dad."

"What kind of parents would want their child to marry into a family unknown to them?" she asked.

"We'll see when the time comes," he replied cryptically, all the while wondering how he was going to explain the 'new world' to his parents.

This development did not sit well with Mutunga's parents. All along he had been a model son but now he was talking gibberish. There simply could not be a true marriage without parental involvement. Indeed, from their point of view, their consent was essential. Kanini's conversation with her son left her wondering whether his behavior was a product of his education. After they bid him good-bye, her husband echoed the same thought,

"Is this what education is doing to young people now?" e'Muthembwa wondered out aloud.

Almost six months after this conversation with his mother, Mutunga and Sue Gilchrist, a white Canadian, decided to drive out into the country to see his parents. The young loving pair was motoring along the pitted, dirt road to his parents' home, when it came into view less than two thousand meters beyond a thick wooded corner. There it was, down a slight incline; the terracotta roofed, red brick house. The sight heightened Mutunga's apprehension. His gut tightened - a change that Sue seemed to sense. She patted his knee lightly.

"I'm sure it's going to be alright," she said reassuringly.

"I hope so," he said without much conviction.

He had chosen a day he knew his parents would be home, having decided first to introduce his fiancée before telling them who he had decided to marry. He wished the distance was longer as the house came closer and closer. It was time to stop and get out of the car.

His parents had heard the car drive up as they sat under a shade tree. They stood up to greet their visitors.

"Dad, Mom. Meet Sue," Mutunga said, as he watched his parents' reaction closely.

Following their custom both father and mother silently shook Sue's offered hand.

"We are pleased you brought someone from your office to visit us," his mother said. "Please, sit down," she added as she shook hands with Sue.

Although Sue did not speak the language of Mutunga's family she understood the gestures of hospitality and her fiancé served as translator. He chose not to interpret the comment about bringing someone from work to Sue. Instead, he waited until all of them sat down for the obligatory tea and then dropped the bomb. He sipped his lukewarm tea, cleared his throat and announced,

"Mum, Dad. Sue and I plan to get married."

Silence.

Several more sips of tea.

His parents were dumbfounded. Tradition had always demanded that one's parents start negotiations with the future in-laws long before any talk of marriage. They never expected their well-bred, and hopefully well-behaved, son would leave them speechless. They had not spied any liquor on his breath and he was not otherwise acting deranged. Thoughts of Matthew, their errant first son, crossed the preacher's mind. Education must have changed Mutunga beyond what they understood. Eventually, the preacher found his voice. "*Ko nguivia kimba ung'ethesya?*"[2] he said cryptically, quoting a tribal proverb. Then he added, "We wish both of you happiness." He thought to himself, "God never gives one a burden one cannot bear" but did not say it aloud. Then the question expressing his father's biggest fear came, "Does Sue's family approve of this marriage?"

"That's wonderful. And yes, her parents do. In fact, they are planning to fly from Canada to attend the wedding ceremony," Mutunga responded with great relief in his voice. "We would be honored if you came too."

The preacher locked eyes with his wife briefly, a question, a visual contact and quick agreement. "Of course it will be a great pleasure to attend your wedding."

Reverend e'Muthembwa was slightly miffed that his son

---

[2] Can I pay for a corpse smart enough to look into the future?

had not asked him to officiate at the ceremony but as he thought more about it he realized there would be a language problem if he were to marry the young couple. He also recognized the familial determination, the desire to forge one's future independently, and the belief in one's surefootedness that reminded him of a young man working on a white owner's coffee farm many years ago. He smiled quietly to himself. "Like father, like son," he thought proudly.

Three months later the preacher and his wife were happy to attend their son's church wedding in Nairobi. Although they did not understand the English words they were able to follow the various steps in the ceremony. It was at this celebration that they finally met Sue's parents. She had learnt enough of her husband's mother tongue to facilitate a simple conversation between the two sets of parents. That deeply impressed e'Muthembwa as well as her parents. "She'll make an excellent wife for our son," he pronounced as he and Kanini got in the taxi provided for their ride home.

The wedding celebration was well catered for and guests had a wonderful time but it left the preacher uneasy. He regarded frontier austerity and frugality to be essential virtues for all good Christians. He saw the celebration as ostentatious and inappropriate for a preacher's son but had the sense to bite his tongue and say nothing. He paid heed to the tribal proverb: 'The mother sheep has no horns.' (Offspring get preferential treatment). After all, his son was now married in a church but more to the point he did not wish to alienate his new daughter-in-law or risk losing his second son.

On thinking back, his logic clouded by his personal understanding of the tenets of his new religion, e'Muthembwa wondered how his first son could have turned

79

out so badly. "It is so hard to know how to guide young people in this modern day and age without losing them completely," he thought to himself. "What could I have done differently? Let us not lose our second son by opposing his marriage to this foreign woman."

SEVEN

IN AS MUCH as he tried to keep it out of his mind, e'Muthembwa often found himself thinking about his failure as a parent. At least that is how he viewed his estrangement from his first son, Matthew, named after the first book of the New Testament.

Before uprooting the rest of the family to Kithongoto, he had entrusted his eldest son to the care of one of his brother who lived close to the intermediate school that the boy attended. That, he expected, would enable the young boy to continue with his schooling. The child had done well in primary school and earned a place in the nearby school. Living with his uncle's family was a huge change for Matthew who had spent his early years in a close-knit and closely supervised family, a family that monitored his daily school activities and nurtured his growth.

By contrast, he found a *laissez-faire* approach to discipline at his uncle's home, a less structured philosophy towards child upbringing and little interest in education. The lack of structure made the boy feel abandoned. In fact, it made him think his parents did not care about him, especially his father. As children sometimes do, he began to think, "Maybe he's not really my father!" Up to the time e'Muthembwa took the rest of the family to go live with him at Kithongoto, he had regularly asked to see the child's school reports but now no one seemed to care or even be interested in what he did.

In intermediate school young Matthew's interest in education began to falter. No one took him to task over his lack of effort; there were no immediate consequences and no encouragement. So long as his father did not see his progress card or accidentally run into any of his teachers, he had nothing to fear. Kithongoto was too far away for casual family visits or for accidental teacher-parent encounters.

Afraid of facing his father at the end of each school term, he got creative in inventing reasons as to why it was better for him to spend the holidays at his uncle's home. Somehow he knew the preacher cared too much about doing well in school to accept any excuses his first son was likely to give regarding his poor school performance.

Messages from the teachers and the headmaster regarding his poor work at school had been sent to Matthew's uncle to no avail. Consequently, his father was none the wiser until the graduation term, three years later, when he made the three-day trip to visit his son's school and learnt that the lying young man had not done well enough to qualify for high school placement.

Although he blamed himself for his son's failure, the preacher made it clear to his brother that he did not think much of his parenting skills. Nonetheless, e'Muthembwa firmly believed his brother's laxity did not excuse his son's lack of effort and harshly rebuked him for it.

"What have you been doing for the past three years?" the preacher thundered. "I'll brook no sloth in my house. We can beg your teachers to allow you to repeat eighth grade. Then you can work for better exam grades. That way you'll then qualify for high school."

"Dad, I don't want to repeat," whined young Matthew.

"So, you're too old to take my advice? In that case, you'd better find a way to support yourself," his father responded in a voice full of anger and disappointment.

He might as well have told his son "he was finished with him," that there was no longer a place for him in his mother's hut.

Not daring to respond to his enraged father, the rebellious son kept silent, but when his father left and without any hesitation or clear view of his future, he signed up to start work as an untrained teacher after completion of intermediate school instead of going on to high school. Fortunately for Matthew this was a time when an eighth grader could still get a teaching position in elementary school.

Matthew had tested his father's affection and found it wanting. The "old man's" reaction confirmed to the young man what he had suspected all along, that e'Muthembwa was not his natural father and that what Matthew did with his own life was of no consequence to his professed father.

His chastised uncle tried half-heartedly to guide the young man who thought that because he was earning a meager salary he was mature enough to face the world on his own terms. It did not take him long to start smoking bhang and enjoying the locally brewed alcoholic beverages. The downward spiral continued as his life changed precipitously when he forced himself on one of his pre-pubescent female students. His crime earned him three and a half years in jail, far away from any of his relatives.

When his father heard the news all he said was, "I've no son by that name." He forbade Kanini from visiting their imprisoned son or ever mentioning his name again. He had named his first child after the saint of the same name; a fact which constantly reminded the preacher of the scriptural admonition in the Gospel of Saint Matthew that if one's eye made one to sin then it should be plucked out. He did not wish to harbor a sinner in his house. Eager to prove to his congregation that he was a man of God, he failed to exercise one of the virtues of his new religion: forgiveness. True to his religious belief the preacher and his first son never became reconciled.

If anyone in Kithongoto knew about the scandal of the preacher's wayward son no one ever mentioned it to e'Muthembwa or Kanini. In all likelihood, no one knew of the existence of the preacher's first son; his parents were quite selective in the information they shared with members of the congregation. True to form, they never again mentioned the name of their errant first son; his existence was not a topic they cared to bruit about.

To the strict preacher, Matthew's incarceration was the final straw, the breaking point when his father decided he had had enough. The preacher in the father could not accept such criminal behavior in his son: being true to his religious beliefs, his calling was more important than tolerating evil even if it meant disowning his son.

Mutunga did not get to know much about his older brother; the family had moved to Kithongoto when he was barely five. He remembered that his brother had been left with their uncle in order for him to continue with his schooling; however, Mutunga had expected his brother to join the family when school was out but that never happened. When he asked his mother about Matthew she gave him a stern look that told Mutunga the subject was forbidden. "Perhaps something awful had happened to him. Did he suddenly die? Surely there would have been a funeral," his young mind thought.

As he got older, his parents acted as if he was their first child since nothing in their home reminded him of his brother. It was not until Mutunga was in a boarding high school, closer to where they had lived, that a classmate mentioned that he had met his older brother. That piqued his curiosity in finding Matthew but it remained a mystery.

During his second year in college, he made up his mind to search for his brother. Mutunga's parents had been completely unhelpful and even obstructive to his efforts by their refusal to talk about Matthew and therefore their denial of his existence. No one was willing to tell him what caused the estrangement. In fact, Mutunga's exploratory attempts to extract information from his mother seemed to annoy as well as frighten her.

To challenge his father was out of the question, as the preacher would never be pushed to talk about something he did not wish to discuss. To avoid alienating his parents he had to be circumspect in his search. That ruled out contacting his uncle or any other relative in his ancestral area since the only way he could do that would be by visiting them and news of a visit would immediately get back to his parents.

In the meantime, Matthew had kept up with his younger brother's progress in school. He knew when he went to college even though he had no idea what Mutunga was studying. He kept his distance because of fear that their father might accuse him of trying to lead his younger brother astray. By the time he gathered enough courage to contact him, Mutunga had already graduated and now Matthew did not know where he had gone. He even wondered whether he would be able to recognize his own brother. So he stopped trying to find him.

The idea of finding Matthew remained at the back of Mutunga's mind as he rushed about looking for employment. When he eventually found a job there was so much to do that he simply did not have time to spare. He often found himself flying overseas or to another African country to take part in some negotiation or make a presentation. The more he got involved in his work the less time he spent thinking about his lost brother and as time passed the urgency of finding him diminished.

What neither of them knew was that they both worked in Nairobi, a not so large city at that time. After serving his time in prison, Matthew stopped drinking and taking drugs and tried different ventures in an effort to eke out a living. Eventually, he started his own business as a curio and wood carvings seller in the city central market. By his second year, he was doing well enough to pay off the debts he had accrued while setting up the business. The quality of the goods he sold had improved considerably by the fourth year of his business and he was planning to expand his sales area.

On a sunny morning in late March, when the weather

turns muggy in the early afternoon and remains unbearably unpleasant for walking about in the crowded city center, two white Canadian tourists, their daughter and her fiancé emerged from the Norfolk Hotel after a late breakfast.

To help digest the big breakfast of hot cereal, pineapple juice, sausages with fried eggs and toast, coffee and a side dish of tropical fruit salad they decided to walk the short distance to the open city market a few blocks down the street. As soon as they entered the walled-off open-air market a rainbow of colors assaulted their eyes and pleasant scents from fresh cut flowers were competing with the stench of open sewer effluence running between the shaded stalls. The cacophony of haggling sellers and buyers announced a vibrant market.

Theirs was not a shopping excursion but a short walk around town before the tourists joined a three-day guided safari in Amboseli National Park later in the day. Past the crowded colorful textile stalls were African woven sisal baskets and beyond those the curios and woodcarvings of various African game animals. Their daughter's fiancé had been bragging about his tribe being the only one which made worthwhile carvings.

"How much do you want for this?" asked the white tourist as he held up a carving of an elephant in the third stall in their path.

"That's one 'undred fifty shillings. It's carved from the core of an ebony tree. One of the best carvings I've ever seen," the seller answered brightly.

"And how much for the rhino?" his wife asked as she cradled another carving.

"One 'undred twenty." Ever the hustler, the man had already identified the couple as husband and wife. "But for the two carvings I'll give you a good price of two 'undred thirty shillings," he offered. "Or, for the two carvings and this African 'air comb I'll let you 'ave them all for two 'undred thirty five only."

He had paid little attention to the young white woman who stood a few paces away from her parents who had come to Kenya to visit her. Sue, the young woman, was a United Nations employee on a two-year contract working in Kenya. She had warned her parents not to pay the first price quoted when buying anything in the market because it was customary to haggle, talk down the price and if they did not like it to walk away.

"How about two hundred for both carvings?" the tourist countered.

"Make it two 'undred twenty and I'll throw in the comb."

Mutunga, who had pretended to be interested in items in the next stall but had been listening to the haggling, exchanged a quick look with Sue, a pre-arranged signal that it was time for him to go rescue her parents. From the haggling he had deduced from the frequency of dropped "hs" in spoken English that the seller was from his own tribe. He walked up and stared at the items in question. He picked up the elephant in order to examine the wood. A quick look confirmed what he suspected: the carving was of some other hard wood which had been polished black in order to simulate ebony. With a firm but friendly tone he addressed the seller in Kikamba, his tribal language,

"This is not ebony. It's covered with black polish."

"They don't know the difference," the seller replied in the same language, nonplussed by the language change and the challenge to his assertion about the provenance of the carving.

"Oh, but *I* know."

"But you're not the one buying. What difference does it make to you?"

"Tell me. What's your name?" Mutunga continued in the same language.

"Matthew."

At the mention of his name something clicked in Mutunga's long suppressed memory but he had to be sure first.

"No. I mean your real Kikamba name."

"That's the name my parents gave me. My father's name is Muthembwa."

At the mention of his father's name Mutunga's jaw dropped then his eyes misted. He stared at the seller, trying to discern some feature he recognized but he was too shaken. The memory of his brother was from almost twenty-eight years before, when Matthew was six or seven years old and much taller than Mutunga was at age five. This man was two or so inches shorter than he, with long untidy hair and dressed in clothes that appeared to have been slept in too many times. He could easily pass for a homeless person who lived out on the streets, a person who one would hesitate to present to one's future in-laws as his long lost brother. Besides, Muthembwa was a common enough name among the Akamba that the seller could be entirely unrelated to him. Then why did he have a Christian name and no Kikamba given name?

Yet, he sensed they had nothing in common. Mutunga was in a quandary; should he ascertain that this man was truly his brother and then be forced to introduce him to his companions or wait for another time? It would reflect poorly on his family, especially taking into account that this Matthew had tried to cheat Sue's parents.

Sue and her parents had been watching this exchange without fully following the conversation. From the expression on Mutunga's face, Sue knew something important was happening. Her fiancé was closely scrutinizing the seller's face and that was very unusual for he normally never showed much interest in how strangers looked. Her inner sense told Sue there was more to their conversation. Could this be the long lost brother he once mentioned? She found herself looking for any resemblance but saw none, which she dismissed as the result of her being a cultural outsider.

Mutunga came back to the present and realized he had been ignoring his company. He continued speaking in the vernacular and dismissively said to the seller,

"If you want them to buy then give the appropriate price and not the tourist one."

"Yes, boss," he said promptly with mock humility. Then in English he continued, "Your friend almost talked me into giving you these wonderful carvings free of charge but I 'ave a business to run. So I'll let you 'ave them for one 'undred sixty and I'll add the comb free. Do I 'ave a sell?"

"Sure," replied Dr. Gilchrist, Sue's father, as he counted bank notes out of his wallet.

The two carvings were quickly but meticulously wrapped and, with thanks, handed over to their new owners.

As they walked away, Sue asked Mutunga, "What did you say to make him lower the price?"

"Oh, just that we're not tourists."

Sue knew that he was not telling the whole story but chose to defer taking him to task until later. The tone in which he answered her question told her something important *had* taken place between the two men and she promised herself that she would find out later at a more propitious time.

It bothered Mutunga that he could not share the news about meeting Matthew with any member of his family, especially his mother. Before they left the market, he swore to himself that he would return alone and have a longer conversation with Matthew in order to find out if he was indeed his brother. This was in spite of his fear that a close relationship with a relative with whom he had so little in common could cause problems in the future.

Unfortunately, he was not able to visit the market for another four months. When he got there, he found Matthew's stall occupied by a woman selling homemade baskets. On inquiring as to the whereabouts of the former occupant of the space, he was told Matthew no longer sold curios at the market; he was now working with an exporter of wood-carvings and traveled throughout the country buying for his business partner. Mutunga could not find anyone who would tell him how to get in touch with the curio seller. He regretted having botched up the chance he had four months earlier.

Had he forever lost his brother?

EIGHT

I HATE YOU! I hate you! I hate you and I'm never coming back," Christopher screamed at his mother as he ran sobbing out of the flat.

Bernadette ran frantically after him, calling to him to come back to no avail. She wasn't fast enough to catch up with her swift thirteen-year-old son. He had run away once before and had come back a few days later, but this time she feared he might not return. She had met his father, Samuel Kimweli, fourteen years earlier when she was looking for a husband. Christopher knew nothing about that.

In a country where barely one third of the youth made it beyond high school, Samuel had a career that set him apart from most of his peers. Not only did he have a university degree, but a high-paying and high-status position in the provincial office. Shortly after his post-graduate training as an agricultural inspector he met Bernadette.

To him, the meeting was pure coincidence; he did not

know that she had already singled him out as a prospective husband. With his new position in the province he was indeed quite a catch for any woman and Bernadette was determined to be the lucky girl who landed the big one. Samuel had first appeared in Bernadette's feminine radar through Doris, her friend and his cousin. Thereafter, Bernadette studied the after-work hangouts of the young man she recognized only from a distance as she plotted her strategy.

One early evening after work, she and her friend conspired to follow him to a local bar, a building one could easily mistake for an old barn. Githuri's Bar and Restaurant was really a bar that served tough roasted goat meat and sometimes soggy French fries. It stocked mainly the local Pilsner and Tusker beers, spirits and mixers as well as Cokes, Pepsis and Fantas. The faded and peeling light brown paint on the outside and the nondescript entrance half-way along one of the longer sides of the 'barn,' in no way complimented the inside décor.

Entering the place, one faced an enlarged, cheaply framed black and white panoramic photograph of a herd of elephants in Amboseli - with the matriarch's ears flared, ready to charge the viewer, Mt. Kilimanjaro looming high in the background - hung on the cream wall to the left of the short curved *mvule* hardwood counter. The well-worn high bar stools were of the same wood, dark-brown with seats shiny from long constant use. Rather ordinary ebony carvings of various African animals were strategically placed around the dimly lit room. Round Formica-topped tables that seated four in low, hard wooden chairs were placed haphazardly around the long room. Short olive- green drapes over single-glazed, louvered windows completed the room decorations.

The two women had planned for Doris to introduce Bernadette to Samuel and then disappear. When they entered the pub they espied Samuel sitting alone at the bar. They casually walked up and ordered two Fantas, each feigning surprise at meeting him.

"Hello, Samuel. I'd like you to meet my friend, Bernadette," Doris, his cousin, breathed out.

"Glad to meet you," Samuel said as he shook hands with Bernadette. His gesture was formal as befitted a new acquaintance. Bernadette lingered letting go of his hand but he thought nothing of it.

"Mind if we join you?" Doris inquired, more as a courtesy as each woman took the bar stool on either side of Samuel.

"Why don't we take a table instead," he suggested.

The trio slid off the bar stools and moved to a nearby table. The conversation drifted into what each did for a living with Bernadette feigning surprise that she had not met him before since she also worked in the neighborhood where the provincial offices were located. When Doris finished her Fanta she excused herself, claiming she had to go baby-sit for her aunt. Samuel noticed that Bernadette seemed to be in no hurry.

"Would you care for another Fanta?" he offered.

"Can I have a gin and tonic?" Bernadette asked.

"I'll stick to my beer," Samuel said as he beckoned the bartender. "A gin and tonic and another cold Pilsner, please."

When the drinks arrived they continued chatting. He found her attractive and thought she was interested in him, but how much he could not tell. Although he missed female company, he was cautious. He knew several of his men friends had been trapped into marriages they did not ask for and did not want to be the next victim.

On the surface he appeared to be a not very serious young man who drank quite a lot, laughed a lot, and socialized with the guys at the bar or the sports club. He had his own definite ideas however, about the kind of woman he would want for a wife: someone who was pretty, but also sensible and practical, preferably with a good education. Someone he would be passionate about and want to pursue until she loved him, too.

As the alcohol took effect the conversation became less guarded.

"Do you have a girlfriend?" Bernadette asked coyly. Of course, she knew the answer but wanted to make sure her intentions were clear.

"Not at the moment," Samuel replied without much enthusiasm.

He did not like being interrogated. He quickly gulped his last mouthful of beer, a gesture that indicated he was ready to leave.

"Then you wouldn't mind coming to our picnic next Saturday – if you're free," Bernadette added. "Doris will give you a call since I don't have a telephone," she lied. "Does she have your number?"

He felt somewhat cornered but chose to ignore his apprehension. As he stood up he reached for his wallet and pulled out one of his newly printed business cards.

"This should do. And thanks for the invite. Sorry I have to run," he said as he turned towards the door.

She did not get up but remained seated, studying Samuel's card as if it was a gold nugget. Now she had a means of getting in touch with him without having to go through her friend. She contentedly sipped her gin and tonic, mulling over her next move. She knew that no picnic had been planned for the following Saturday. Besides, she wanted Samuel all to herself. She had three days to come up with a credible alternative.

The following day, two days before the expected picnic, she called Samuel from her office. She had already conferred with Doris who had planned a weekend visit to her parents' home out in the country.

"Doris is unwell so we postponed the picnic. Instead, I'm inviting you to lunch at Kristo's on Saturday."

"That's fine, provided I get to pay my way."

"We'll see about that. Shall we meet at one p.m?"

"One o'clock is fine."

"See you the day after tomorrow at one, then."

As Bernadette hung up she had a warm feeling. Everything was going according to her plan.

Kristo's was a small, cozy restaurant situated in the town suburbs on a short side street off one of the main roads from the town center. With its manicured gardens and shade trees its terrace eating area presented the perfect laid back experience in outdoor dining. Full-grown white acacia trees provided ample and cool shade over the bricked circular areas where the tables were set with light-blue linen napkins. A high clay fountain was set in one of the far corners of the grounds. On cool or rainy days one dined inside the one-storey building with its picture windows running almost the entire wall that faced the outside eating area. The dining room was illuminated by sconces along the inside wall and on the heavy pillars between the windows.

On several occasions Samuel had been served some of Kristo's excellent French, Italian or Greek meals; it was one of his favorite restaurants. He found himself looking forward to his lunch date, his hesitation overcome by the thought of a scrumptious lunch and the quiet ambiance he treasured at Kristo's. He realized, too, that his long drought of female intimacy was beginning to influence his thoughts.

Late Saturday morning he showered, shaved and dressed in a light-brown, short-sleeved cotton shirt with matching dark-brown cotton-linen trousers and brown sandals, the perfect casual outfit for his thirty-one year-old, trim, six-foot frame. He made sure his short hair was properly combed. He tried to visualize the face of the woman he had met only once. Her face had not been striking, he recalled, but she had an attractive mouth and when she smiled her round face broke into dimples. The light at the bar had not been bright enough to afford him a clear description of her eyes. He would find out soon enough.

He timed himself to arrive at the restaurant shortly after one o'clock. When he did, he found Bernadette already seated at a corner table, under the dappled shade of one of the large acacia trees in the garden. As he approached her table she stood up. In her sleeveless low-cut red dress that showed off her delicate twenty-five year-old feminine neck she oozed feminine charm. For the first time, he noticed her near perfect figure, full hips and pert breasts taunting him. Her brown flirty eyes peered mischievously at him from her round face. Neither was sure of what to do next, shake hands or hug. Instead, they both sat down.

"I wasn't sure you'd come," she said as they studied the menu.

"I said I would, didn't I?" he countered rather gruffly.

"I'm glad you did," she said sweetly.

"I wouldn't miss a meal at this place for anything."

As soon as the waiter came over they each ordered a

steak entrée with a glass of red house wine. All the while, Bernadette was studying his angular face, his kind brown eyes that belied their mocking laughter, pausing to appreciate Samuel's strong masculine jaw. She imagined kissing his full lips, but her daydreaming was interrupted by the arrival of their food.

"Enjoy," the waiter said as he departed.

Very little was said until about halfway through the meal when the conversation picked up. They chatted about their work and anything else that came to mind. Samuel found out that Bernadette was a devout Catholic and this gave him pause. Catholic girls were not known for being easy and he knew he was not ready for marriage. As if she was reading his mind, Bernadette asked,

"What do you think of marriage?"

"That's a heavy one. Besides, I hardly know you," he stated cautiously but with a subtle smile. "As for the institution itself, I'm all for it. But I'm not sure I'm ready for it yet."

"I wasn't asking you to marry me," she chided playfully as she smiled back at him.

They continued to banter until the end of the meal. When he called for the bill she was in no hurry to settle it. Bernadette did not object when Samuel put down enough cash to cover the cost of both lunches and the tip.

"Thank you very much for the treat," she said as the waiter picked up the money. Samuel was rather surprised she did not offer to pay at least her tab since she was the one who invited him, but thought little of it. He didn't really mind paying as he was enjoying female company for a change. His work kept him so busy that he seldom went out on a date.

At that point Samuel suggested they take a walk in the

gardens. He knew there were park benches where they could sit, away from the other diners and continue getting acquainted. They got up, headed for the gardens and picked the bench farthest from the dining tables. They sat with only a few inches separating them, facing the winding path along which they had arrived. Their voices acquired a conspiratorial tone as they stared into each other's eyes. Samuel was thinking a short fling with her would be fun and was ready to move to the next step but he was dubious whether the Catholic Bernadette would countenance his being so forward on a first date. To his surprise, he noticed her breathing had changed; it was now deep yet rapid. He had the impression she was sliding towards him as he moved towards her. A quick touching of lips and the moment was over.

"I think we should leave," Bernadette said quietly. She didn't want to appear too easy, for fear of scaring him away. She was planning on more than just a one-night stand.

They slowly stood up and walked side by side towards a side entrance to the restaurant grounds. As the parking area came into view, Samuel asked,

"Would you care for a ride to your flat?"

"No thanks. I've errands I need to run before returning home."

He realized he had no quick way of getting in touch with her since at their initial meeting she had mentioned that she did not have a telephone. All he had was a general idea of where she lived. Before panic set in, Bernadette reached out and held Samuel's hand. Looking intently into his eyes, she asked alluringly,

"Can I call you on Monday?"

"That'd be great. I won't be doing any field work, so should be in the office most of the day," he quickly responded, grateful for the lifeline she had tossed out to him.

Thus ended their first date.

By the third date, two weeks later, their relationship had advanced to kisses and wild groping in the car while on a drive out in the country. It would have become more intimate if the setting had been different. The fourth date was a drive in Samuel's car through the nearby game park after which Bernadette indicated she wanted to see where Samuel lived. That was what he had been hoping for; he was at the point where anything short of full intimacy left him feeling frustrated. When they arrived at Samuel's flat, Bernadette asked where the bathroom was and disappeared, shortly to reappear shoeless in the sitting room -- all cheery and expectant.

"Can I see where you sleep?" she asked demurely.

"Through that door," he pointed while he remained seated in the sofa near the door to his dining room, wrestling with his fear of entrapment.

Bernadette glanced at the door but make no move towards it. Instead, she gave Samuel the come-hither look, her eyes challenging him to follow her into the bedroom. His arousal betrayed his resolve as he got up. He put his arm around her waist and both walked awkwardly into the bedroom. Even then he was concerned she might get pregnant. As they kissed and undressed each other, Samuel stopped suddenly.

"Are you protected or should I get something else?" he asked her in a husky voice.

"I'm fine," she replied, briefly breaking away from kissing his neck.

Afterwards, they lay quietly next to each other for a while, each trying to understand the full meaning of what had just taken place between them. He eventually dozed off and woke up to find Bernadette running the tips of her fingers along the inside of his thighs. He realized he was already aroused again as she straddled him. After it was over they got up and showered together, sharing the same towel, and got dressed. During the drive to her home neither said much. Their intimate relationship had started, with Samuel expecting it to be a stopgap friendship before he started to look seriously for a wife.

About three months after that day, they had finished eating a picnic lunch in the town arboretum. Bernadette was sitting near the edge of the blanket they had spread for their meal, her back leaning against the trunk of a large fig tree. Her lover lay on his back, diagonally across the blanket with his head resting on her lap, dozing off while he digested realizing his meal – the perfect tableau of a young couple in love, enjoying a quiet moment in the peace of the relaxing greenery. They had not yet repacked their picnic basket.

"Darling, I've something I need to tell you," she cooed.

"Yes. What?" he asked, hardly awake.

"Please don't be angry with me," she continued as she gazed apprehensively at his face.

"Alright."

"I'm pregnant with our child."

Her remark made him sit up, fully awake, the peaceful illusion shattered. He had little reason to doubt that he was indeed the father; she had hardly had time to date other men during the intervening months.

"What? You told me you were protected?" he fumed.

"I was then, but I thought it was about time we began to think about getting married," she replied.

"Wh... What? You thought? We never even discussed ma... marriage!" he exclaimed incredulously. He was so surprised and furious he was stammering.

"But we've been acting the same as married people. Why shouldn't we get married?" she countered, her voice a shade louder than normal.

"People marry for different reasons. In my book pregnancy is not one of them," he yelled. "This is entrapment and I won't put up with it!"

Then he calmed down a little and said, "I'll help raise the baby but I'm not marrying you."

Bernadette's hopes for marrying him were dashed to the ground by his reaction and she in turn became enraged, displaying a side of her personality he had never imagined.

"You depraved heathen. You pretended to love me when all you wanted was to satisfy your dirty animal lust."

He tried to reason with her but Bernadette, realizing suddenly her plot to trap him into marrying her had flopped, became unhinged; throwing anything she could lay her hands on and screaming,

"Don't bother. I don't ever want to see you again! I can raise my *own* child. Get lost you worthless son-of-a-bitch!"

With her final salvo she got up, grabbed her handbag, and stomped away towards the arboretum gate. He was too stunned and angry to care about what happened to her or how she was going to get home. He let her go while he gathered the few unbroken items and cleaned up the mess she had created.

When he felt a bit of compunction and tried to get in touch with her a week later, he found she had moved and no one would tell him where she had gone. He was relieved rather than disappointed because he really did not want her as his wife.

NINE

URING THE INTERVENING period Bernadette had kept track of Samuel's whereabouts. By then the child had been born and grown into a five-year-old boy named Christopher. As a single mother, Bernadette was having trouble making ends meet so she sent a message through his cousin, requesting financial help. His cousin also conveyed Bernadette's adamant insistence that the young boy now needed a father. In essence, she had not given up the fantasy of marrying Samuel, especially as neither had married in the past years.

What Bernadette didn't know was that three years after breaking up with her, Samuel had met a quiet, soft-spoken, well-educated and beautiful woman while giving a seminar. Twenty-six year-old Priscilla Katee had impressed him with her quick but sensitive wit; even when teasing someone she seemed aware of other people's feelings. Her small stature, delicate features and kind brown eyes belied an inner strength that he came to admire. She always seemed to be at peace with the world.

At the beginning of their courtship, Samuel had been the "pursuer" and had been delighted when she eventually told him she had hoped from the first time they met that he would pursue a relationship with her. He adored her and they were now engaged. He and Priscilla, with whom he had already shared details of his encounter with Bernadette, were planning to get married that year and had already asked Reverend e'Muthembwa to officiate at their wedding. When Samuel's former lover contacted him through his cousin as her emissary, he and Priscilla agreed that Samuel should offer Bernadette financial help and no more. Bernadette would have none of it.

Subsequent requests from her, through various intermediaries, got the same reply: if she needed money Samuel was ready to help. Just before Samuel and Priscilla's wedding Bernadette threatened to disrupt the ceremony with claims he was already married. Fortunately, she did not follow through. Samuel was immensely relieved thinking that was the end of being harassed by Bernadette. He expected now that he was married she would leave him alone and he could lead a peaceful life with his chosen wife.

Bernadette disappeared for another six years, years during which their growing son was constantly asking about his father. Christopher was determined to identify his biological father among the men who visited his mother's flat over recent years.

All he was able to extract from his bitter mother were inadequate answers such as, "I'm your father and mother" or angry responses informing him that his father was dead. Her tone of voice belied her statements and only made young

Christopher angry and frustrated. His schoolwork began to suffer as he lost interest in his studies and began running in bad company and sniffing glue. By his twelfth birthday, Christopher felt so alienated from his mother that he ran away from home but came back three days later, unkempt, hungry and tired.

The last straw for him was when he returned home early from school on his thirteenth birthday to find his mother in bed with one of her "gentleman" friends. He furiously threw a clay pot at them and ran out of the flat screaming, "I hate you. I hate you and I'm never coming back." He did return, however, more than a week later, unwashed and reeking of pot.

Bernadette's panic knew no bounds. Unable to afford a telephone, she sent the following note to Samuel.

Dear Sam,

> *I'm writing this letter to plead with you to help me control Christopher. It's the least you can do for your son. His school progress is in retrograde and he is keeping bad company.*
>
> *I can't seem to get him to do anything right. Last time I tried he ran away and did not come home for almost ten days! I'm at my wits end.*
>
> *He needs his father. Kindly tell your cousin when you will come to my home to have a talk with Chris and fulfill your parental duty.*

Sincerely,

Bernadette.

By now, Samuel and Priscilla had built a firm egalitarian marriage. Priscilla was an innate planner and manager. Nothing ruffled her calm demeanor and both husband and wife were strongly committed to their life together. Two years into their marriage, they had started their own family and now had two children. Theirs was a close-knit, happy family.

As Samuel read Bernadette's note the grim expression on his face betrayed his feelings. After being shut out in the raising of their child for so long he was in no mood for games.

His response was curt and to the point:

Bernadette,

> *I'm through with your games. I want nothing to do with you or your son. Don't ever bother me again.*
>
> *Yours truly,*
>
> *Samuel.*

He was ready to send his angry, terse reply after sharing it with Priscilla, who was shocked by the tone of the note.

"You *can't* send this!" she said to her husband.

"And why not?" Samuel retorted, his anger boiling over.

"Because by doing so you are punishing your son for his mother's problems and your own past mistakes," Priscilla answered, more calmly than she felt at that moment.

"She can't shut me out for thirteen years and suddenly expect me to be polite," Samuel blurted out, his irascible temper getting the better of him.

"Well, if you love me you won't send that note," his wife declared.

Her response shocked him into silence and after tempers had cooled down, he quietly asked her,

"What do you think I should do?"

"I think *we* should both pay Bernadette a visit in order to work out a way to help your son," she replied. She had learnt a few tricks by watching and listening to Reverend e'Muthembwa deal with various committee members in his church.

"Alright, that sounds workable," he said, giving her a kiss and thinking how wise she was.

Thus the rescue plan was set into motion.

On the agreed time and day, husband and wife went to Bernadette's flat. She was not home but her son was studiously tackling his school homework. While Samuel and Priscilla waited, he started quizzing young Christopher about his school, examining his workbook to see how he had fared in previous exercises. The father was impressed by the young man's mathematical acuity. For the sensitive and observant Christopher, this was quite a break from the "uncles" who frequented the flat he shared with his mother. None of the previous visitors had shown any interest in his schoolwork.

When his mother eventually came home, the discussion among the three adults yielded little progress. Bernadette still insisted Samuel come alone to her flat to counsel their son, an option which was fraught with devious implications and totally unacceptable to Samuel and Priscilla. On the other hand, she would not entertain the idea of Christopher living with his father. In the end, they all agreed that Bernadette would get a monthly stipend from Samuel, to be delivered by his wife. This way he would not have to talk to Bernadette and it would emphasize that their relationship had ended years before.

The arrangement worked for the first month, but on the second, Christopher caught his mother receiving money from "the woman who had visited their home only twice." He knew the stranger was not one of his mother's friends and therefore started asking questions.

"Mother, why did that woman give you money?"

"Oh, she's just a friend helping us out," Bernadette replied.

"I don't believe you. I know all your friends, so don't lie to me!" he countered.

From the boy's tone, Bernadette knew if she did not come clean she ran the risk of losing him forever. She took a deep breath and set her son down. Through tears and self-recriminations for not telling him sooner she told him who his father was. To her surprise, he remained silent and said no more about it throughout the following year.

On his fifteenth birthday, the young man came home from school, did his homework and waited for his mother to return from work. Like many fifteen year-olds he had been chafing under his mother's rules which to him seemed arbitrary. Even worse, they were inconsistent with her own lifestyle of doing whatever she pleased, staying out late, drinking, and entertaining male visitors. Their meals together were haphazard and he often had to scrounge up something on his own. He knew by hearsay that his father's house was a well-run Christian non-drinking household.

"I've decided to go live with my father," he announced.

"Stop talking nonsense," his mother chided. "You don't even know where he lives."

"I can find out."

"You're not going to leave this flat. That's my final word."

"I'm old enough to decide where to live and I'm finished living in this place where I never know if you'll be home or who I will find here! If you don't let me go to my father, I'll run away and never come back," the boy threatened.

"I forbid it. Now, go to bed." Her voice had the finality that declares the subject is now closed.

The following day the boy did not go to school. After his mother had gone to work in the morning, he simply left the home he shared with her. He took nothing but the clothes on his back and did not return that evening, or the following day. By the third day Bernadette was frantic; she had contacted all her friends and nearby relatives, none of whom had seen Christopher. She called Samuel's house to report this development and she explained the conversation that led to the boy's disappearance. No one knew where to start looking for the runaway in the large town. It was agreed that when he returned Bernadette should call Samuel and he and his wife would come over to talk to the boy.

Almost a week later, Christopher appeared at his father's house, filthy beyond recognition and famished. He reeked of pot and had obviously been drinking alcohol. Fortunately, Priscilla was home with their children. She invited him in without asking any questions and told her oldest child, a boy eleven years old, to find a towel and show Christopher where the shower was. She took some of her husband's clean clothes and offered them to the young man.

"Change into these after your shower," she told him gently.

"Thanks," he said softly as he took the clothes and followed his younger guide to the shower. A warm meal was waiting for him when he came out.

"Eat something while we wait for your father to come home from work," his stepmother said warmly. She did not notify the boy's mother as to his whereabouts, she felt that such action should be left to her husband's discretion.

As soon as Samuel came home, he sent a messenger to let Bernadette know that Christopher had turned up at his home. He suggested they meet to decide what the next step should be. Samuel noticed Christopher was quietly talking with their children who were anxious to show him around their home. He called the young man aside and asked him what he wanted to do. At the same time Samuel made sure Christopher understood that whatever choice he made, his father's feelings towards him would remain the same: he loved him and always would.

"I want to stay with you," Christopher adamantly declared. "And if you make me go live with my mother I'll run away *again*," he added.

"I see," his father said calmly as he tried to hide his concern. "We have to let your mother know your decision."

"She won't agree and I don't want to see her. So please don't let her know I'm here!" his son protested.

"All the same, she has to know. In fact, she's on her way here now."

"Then I'm leaving," the young man exclaimed in a panic as he eyed the front door.

"Don't worry. She cannot physically carry you out of my house. Let me talk to her. You go back to whatever you were doing with the other children."

A distraught but combative Bernadette shortly knocked on the door. After sitting down, she did not immediately ask where Christopher was; in fact her first question was more to the point.

"What shall we do with him? I cannot let him leave home," she burst out in exasperation with a voice worn with worry. Circles around her eyes betrayed several nights spent without sleep.

"He's already run away twice. Obviously your strategy is not working," Samuel commented dryly.

"I'm his mother. He has to come home," Bernadette, said, a note of uncertainty creeping into her voice.

"Then as his mother, let us give him the chance to do that on his own. Give him a day or so," Samuel suggested.

"He's too young to know what he's doing," the boy's mother protested angrily.

"That may be so, but we can't ignore the fact that he's run away twice," Samuel insisted. "If you force him to come with you now he'll only run away again. Then we'll be back where we were, if he ever shows up again."

"Alright, but you'd better make sure he comes home before the two days are up," she said, all of sudden assuming an accusatory tone.

She seemed disorientated and on the verge of tears as she got up and walked to the front door, ignoring the tea Priscilla had served her. She let herself out. Bernadette was in no mood to speak with her son at that moment. Samuel followed and closed the door behind her. As he turned his wife observed,

"You handled that wonderfully. I love you." She gave him a quick hug.

Three days later, Bernadette's brother and uncle visited Samuel's home, as traditional spokesmen for her family, demanding that he "undo" whatever spell he had cast on "their son." If he did not do as they demanded they were prepared to sue him.

Samuel called Christopher into the room and reiterated the promise he had given the young man when he first arrived,

"Where you live is your choice. I'll love you the same regardless of the choice you make. But tomorrow I must send you to your mother so I can't be accused of holding you prisoner."

"You have bewitched the boy," the uncle interjected. "You have until tomorrow evening to bring him home," he demanded.

After Bernadette's relatives left Samuel and Priscilla decided that the best thing was to return Christopher to his mother's home.

In deference to cultural norms, Christopher had not said anything when his mother's relatives made their demands; it was rude for a child to confront adults. He waited until the next afternoon while his stepmother was driving him to his mother's flat when he suddenly tried to jump out of the moving vehicle. Anticipating such action, Priscilla had engaged the automatic locks on all the doors.

On arrival at his mother's flat they found her waiting. It was on a Saturday. Christopher walked past her and went straight into his room. His stepmother neither said a word nor entered the flat; she turned the car round and left. Later that afternoon Christopher reemerged from his room to confront his unyielding mother.

"You cannot keep me here. I'm going to live at my

father's house and if you stand in my way I'll knock you over. *So get out of the way!"* he shouted.

The wild, almost deranged, look on the young man's face was enough to scare his mother. She allowed him to walk out, past the gate in the fence surrounding the large residential building and out into the street towards Samuel's house. Christopher walked the four miles between his mother and father's homes and never looked back.

Late that evening when, for the second time in his young life, he knocked on the front door of his father's home, his stepmother opened the door. She hugged Christopher and then called her husband. They quickly rearranged their children's sleeping setup to allow for one more.

To their delight and amazement, the other children happily accommodated Christopher, immediately treating him as if he was their oldest sibling who had lived with them all their short lives.

The parents' joy was complete when they realized Christopher's interest in school had returned; his grades showed remarkable improvement. The only dark cloud in his new life was the thought of his mother showing up for Parents' Day at the boarding high school his stepmother and father had selected for him. He categorically forbade his mother from coming to the school and when she did not heed his wishes he hid from her.

Four years after he entered high school, Christopher did so well in the exams that he was awarded a scholarship and a place at the university. Three and a half years after he was admitted to university, Christopher graduated with an honors degree in engineering!

At the young man's graduation, Priscilla said a quiet prayer and thanked the old preacher, e'Muthembwa, for all the counseling he had given her when she was growing up and above all, for convincing her father that both boys and girls needed to go to school.

TEN

JOHN NORTH KNEW that people often winced when he shook hands with them, but he was determined to always have a firm handshake because he believed it was a sign of good character. His disposition to honesty was written all over his face and demeanor. His slightly curly reddish blond hair and blue eyes bore testimony to a trace of Irish in his ancestry, borne out by frankness in his words sometimes bordering on rudeness.

As he wrote notes for the mission meeting in Philadelphia, he mused, "I wonder what happened to that preacher in Mulango who suddenly disappeared and hasn't been heard from since."

Preacher Timothy Muthengi had been a firebrand, drawing people to his church from miles around to attend his hellfire and brimstone sermons. The African Inland Mission in Kenya had been very pleased with him, as it was unusual for a Kenyan preacher to attract such a large following in an animist culture within a sparsely populated area.

As John got ready to leave for the mission meeting his wife called from the kitchen,

"Honey, would you please pick up some French bread and liver pâté on your way home?"

"Of course, sweetheart," he answered. "I should be home by five thirty. See you later."

Whilst putting on his coat in the vestibule, he noticed a post card from one of his young friends recently gone out to the mission in Kenya, giving news of recent happenings and a short account of the adjustments he had to make. The postcard made John think of the change in their meals since returning from Kenya seven years ago.

They had been pioneer missionaries in that country for twenty years and while there had eaten the same food as the Kenyans: *ugali* (a paste-like basic food made from white corn meal) as well as corn and various kinds of beans, sometimes enhanced with boiled greens or with goat meat or chicken stew on the rare occasions when these were available. Now they were eating French bread and liver pâté!

After an inspiring meeting and prayers with the new volunteers who would go to Africa to convert and train new preachers, he walked down the street to the bakery and noticed a familiar face among the people waiting in line at the very popular place for artisan bread.

"Mark?!" he exclaimed. "What a pleasant surprise. It's many years since I last saw you. How long has it been? What are you doing these days?"

John noticed that the Kenyan was impeccably dressed, in contrast to his own Sears-bought suit.

"John?" Mark exclaimed, as he reached to grasp the firm hand of his old friend. "It *is* indeed a pleasant surprise. I didn't know you lived in this city. How are Jean and the boys?"

"Jean is well and both of us are now living close to our mother church here in Philadelphia. The boys are married, each with three children of their own."

"It's almost thirty years since I saw them! Our two boys are already out of the nest and sometimes Theresa and I find the house all too quiet. We settled here nearly fifteen years ago after I completed my doctoral studies."

"How time flies!"

"Yes, it certainly does."

"We should get together sometime soon and catch up," John suggested. "Jean would be delighted."

"That would be wonderful, presumably on a Friday evening or anytime on Saturday. Our jobs keep us rather busy during the week," Mark replied. "Would a week this Saturday for lunch at our house be OK? We live about twenty minutes from here. Of course I'll check with Theresa."

"Please do. Now that I've retired we are relatively free."

As they exchanged business cards John noticed that Mark had earned a doctorate and was now assistant director at a local scientific research laboratory. At that point it was their turn to be served and their excited conversation stopped abruptly. But on the way out Mark called out,

"Either Theresa or I will call within the week to confirm the date."

"I'm looking forward to it," John said.

As he hurried to his American-made station wagon, John's thoughts drifted back to when he, as a young missionary in Kenya, first met Mark when he was a barefoot teenager in shorts recently out of the middle school at Kithongoto. He had been instrumental in keeping the young man in the church through his boarding high school days. When Mark was doing his bachelor's degree at New York State University in Buffalo, they had corresponded regularly until he graduated, and then the letters petered out. They lost contact.

Three years after Mark's graduation, John had heard from a mutual acquaintance that Mark was back in Kenya and had recently married Theresa, a Catholic. A few weeks later, the newlyweds had invited John and Jean for supper soon after their wedding. The evening had gone much better than he had anticipated; he had been apprehensive because Mark had married outside his denomination. Theresa was a university graduate but of the Catholic faith and the latter caused John some concern.

Now he was excitedly looking forward to sharing his latest news with Jean, a woman whose body showed little of her age of around sixty years.

"You will not believe who I ran into at the bakery," he almost shouted as he kissed his wife.

"Who?" Jean asked, running her fingers through her short-cropped sun-bleached hair.

"You remember Mark Mulandi from Machakos?"

"Of course I do."

"He and Theresa now live here! He invited us for lunch a week this Saturday. Either he or Theresa will call to confirm and set the time. You should've seen him; he looks healthy and spiffy. He's obviously done well for himself. Here's his card."

"Mmmh. A Ph.D. and assistant director of the lab. I always thought he would turn out OK. They live in the snooty part of town too," Jean said as she looked at the address on the card, an address in one of the wealthy suburbs of Philadelphia.

Theresa was thrilled with the news that Mark had run into their missionary friend from Kenya, that he had extended a lunch invitation to him and his wife. During the twenty years they had lived in the United States, they had made few close friends and rarely entertained at home. Often, they were either traveling on business or too tired to spend time preparing for company. They truly looked forward to their annual two weeks of vacation during which they always went somewhere for a well-earned rest.

"I'll call them this weekend," Theresa said brightly as she placed their friend's business card on the table.

"I hope they drink wine with their meals," Mark said with an amused expression on his face.

"We'll find out soon, won't we?"

"You can always ask when you talk to them," he suggested, a wicked smile on his face.

"No, I'll leave that to you. You know them better."

As John and Jean drove along West Chester Pike, heading northwest towards Newtown Square, each was silently wondering about what they would find at the end of their thirty-minute drive. Theresa had given Jean detailed directions to her and Mark's home. The missionary couple previously had little need to drive around this particular neighborhood. Each turn in the road revealed only full grown trees lining the streets with individual houses set back in

what appeared to be quadruple-size lots. A few more blocks
on they found Ivy Lane and several houses later pulled into
the curved driveway of a two-storey, red brick house with a
manicured garden and a two-car garage set to one side. The
cemented-pebble driveway ended in a wide turning circle in
front of the two-car garage door.

John let out a soft whistle. "I wonder how much they
paid for this?" he thought out aloud.

"It's impressive," Jean added quietly.

From the backside garden, Mark had heard their visitors
drive up. He appeared from the side of the house away from
the garage entrance with a bouquet of sunset-colored roses in
his hand.

"Welcome! Jean, I haven't seen you in ages," he said as
he embraced her lightly. He shook hands with John, prepared
to counter the hard squeeze he remembered so well. He was
not disappointed; John gave him a hearty squeeze. Pointing
to the flowers Mark added, "Theresa asked me to get these
for the table. Please come in."

He led them to the stained glass front door and let the
couple in. To them it seemed palatial, a spacious entryway
leading to a large seating room with a formal dining room off
to the left. The high cathedral ceiling was finished with the
beams partially visible, almost shiny with a light wood stain
contrasting with the white color between them. A wide floor-
to-ceiling window led the eye to a small fountain outside the
semi-secluded part of a terraced garden which seemed to
extend down to the thick woods almost a hundred meters
from the back of the house. Outside and off to the left of the
window, John and Jean noticed a wind-protected deck with a
table set for four. Each place setting at the table had water
and wine glasses.

It was that time of the year when outdoor dining is most comfortable.

Just then, Theresa appeared from the kitchen, wiping her hands on a towel which she threw onto the dining table as she came to greet their visitors.

"Jean! John! I never thought I would see you again," she said excitedly as she hugged each.

"You have a wonderful home," Jean observed.

"Oh. Thank you. I'll give you a quick tour," Theresa said as she led them towards her home office. The house had four bedrooms, two of which they had converted into offices.

By the time Theresa finished her tour Mark had already arranged the flowers and set them at the center of the table on the deck. Theresa led the couple to the deck through the family room with its flat-screen television and sound system. Classical music was playing in the background.

"Here we are. Get comfortable while I get the food out," Theresa said as she ushered them towards the cushioned wicker furniture set in the corner of the deck they had not seen from inside the house. The view was pleasant and relaxing.

"I could stay here the rest of my life," John said quietly to his wife.

"It's peaceful," she observed. They had been married for so long that she knew he was simply admiring the view and not feeling jealous of their hosts.

With the help of the three-times-a-week maid, Theresa and Mark quickly brought out the lunch dishes: marinated grilled chicken breast in white sauce with green pepper corns, baked potatoes and green salad. A cold pitcher of lemonade, another of iced water and an open bottle of chilled pinot grigio in its own cooler completed the presentation.

"The guinea fowl is cooked to the tail," Mark announced, using a proverb from his culture to which John and Jean were privy.

"I haven't heard that one used for years," John beamed.

When each was settled and Theresa was serving their plates, Mark broached the question of what to drink. The missionaries had preached abstinence from alcohol while in Kenya but he was uncertain as to what they had with their meals in America. So he chose his words carefully, he did not want to offend their guests. With as little fanfare as he could manage he said,

"The meal goes really well with a glass of chilled, light wine. Jean, John would you like to see how it tastes? Of course there's lemonade and also water."

"I'll have the wine, please," Theresa interjected.

Mark pulled the pinot grigio out of the cooling container and half-filled Theresa's glass.

"John?"

"I'll try a fourth of what Theresa has." Jean gave him a surprised quizzical look as Mark dribbled a few drops into John's glass.

"Jean?"

"I'll have the lemonade," she replied firmly.

About ten minutes into the meal John commented the wine did go well with the meal, but when he finished his eighth of a glass he asked for water instead. Light but animated conversation, catching up on old news, continued throughout the meal until the maid brought out the fruit salad for dessert. Between mouthfuls, John asked,

"Mark, I was talking recently to one of our missionaries in your area and he told me one of our original firebrand preachers had left the church and disappeared from the radar of the Christian community in the eastern parts of Ukambani. You know that part of the country well. Might you know what happened to pastor Timothy Muthengi?"

Mark swallowed hard. He really did not know how to explain what had happened to the pastor without embarrassing John and Jean.

Muthengi, the ascetic preacher, had taken the biblical truth telling to its most basic level. He believed one should never use euphemisms or half-truths in describing one's sins while asking God for forgiveness. He spoke with the frankness of a child.

When he left all his family behind to go and minister to the people in eastern Ukambani, he was known for his fervent belief in the power of prayer. Once he prayed to God "to dry up an orange tree" next to the church building because noisy kids were interrupting his sermons while they picked the fruit. For some reason the tree dried up within two weeks! The locals were afraid of angering him lest he ask God to smite them.

With such a reputation the people dared not challenge his interpretation of the scriptures. They tolerated his idiosyncratic behavior and many joined his new congregation out of curiosity but they were bewildered that a preacher could be as crude as Timothy was at times. Pastor Timothy Muthengi was a semi-literate preacher who had failed to reconcile traditional etiquette with tenets of the new religion and did not realize that one did not necessarily supplant the other. In truth he did not fully understand Christianity as practiced in western societies where common courtesy constrains believers' language in describing their sins and convictions. If his behavior was a model of followers of the new religion then it was only a matter of time before the locals decided to ditch Christianity and revert to their traditional animistic beliefs.

Mark cleared his throat and wished he still smoked the pipe; it would have bought him time to organize his thoughts. Instead he took a small sip of wine, quietly swirled it his mouth and swallowed.

"Do you know the meaning of his given tribal name, Muthengi?" Mark, with a subtle smile on his face, asked no one in particular. He was stalling, uncertain as to how he was going answer the question.

"The drunkard," Jean volunteered.

"Well, that's what he was the last time I saw him. His is a long story, I'm afraid," Mark said.

"What made him go back to the old ways?" John wondered aloud.

"How well did you know him?" Mark asked.

"I met him briefly once or twice. I know he was converting people left and right. At the time, he had one of the largest congregations in that part of Ukambani," John explained.

"You probably know the local chief had donated the piece of land on which the church was built," Mark continued. "In fact, the chief was among Timothy's initial converts. The whole family had joined the church, three wives and several offspring. Overall, I believe the family swelled the initial congregation by fifteen or so.

"Timothy was needling the chief to divorce his last two wives, an act which would have been against tradition. It would have been a meaningless and unkind gesture, as seen by the community and a loss of status on the part of the chief. The friction between the two proud men caused the chief to have second thoughts about the new religion. In addition, Timothy's sometime abrasive words did not endear him to the chief.

"One Sunday morning the congregation, as usual, was making its weekly confessions out loud during the service. The usual sins were aired and the congregation fell silent. What followed shocked everyone and made the chief furious. It was so graphic that it makes me uncomfortable telling it. The service was at the juncture where normally the pastor would pray to God for forgiveness of all who had sinned during the week. Instead, Pastor Timothy Muthengi cleared his throat and in his sonorous tenor voice declared,

"'I, too, have a confession to make.'

"This made everyone in the congregation look up at him. So, he continued,

"'Last night, in my dreams, I sinned. I dreamt that I was in bed with the chief's beautiful daughter, the one sitting right there. (His right pointing finger extended toward the now embarrassed young woman.) In my dream she sat up and hiked up her skirt and she had no other garments under-neath. She then mounted my member and started working her hips. She bumped and ground until I ejaculated. I ask God for His forgiveness. Now, let us pray.'

"When he pointed at the chief's daughter the outraged father walked out. As for the rest, no one dared look up; all eyes were cast downward. The congregation was numb. The preacher had dared break taboo: traditionally, there are topics one never talks about in mixed age and company. This was one.

"When the prayer was over, one by one, the entire con-gregation got up silently and left. They did not wait for the collection to be made. Pastor Muthengi found himself alone in the church, unaware that he had ruined the reputation of the chief's daughter and insulted the community. He had sealed the fate of his young parish and that marked the end of his missionary work."

John sat still, looking with half-closed eyes towards the trees at the edge of the sloping garden. For once he did not have a quick follow-up to make. Jean's face was the color of someone who had sat out in the sun for too long, her lips showing the expression of someone who had just swallowed a bitter pill. Theresa knew the story so her reaction was muted. Mark wondered whether he had gone too far.

Addressing the missionary couple, Mark added quietly, "I hope you don't blame me for telling you the sordid story. I thought you would want to know. Isolation is what drove poor Timothy to drink."

"Anyone care for tea or coffee?" Theresa inquired, in her effort to break the tension. As a gracious host she was eager to change the subject.

"I'll have decaf coffee, no cream," Jean replied.

"Same for me," John added.

"How about you, love?" Mark inquired of Theresa as he got up.

"The usual. Tea with everything," she replied, giving him a tender glance and squeezing his hand.

When Mark returned from the kitchen with the beverages, Jean was asking Theresa about the neighborhood in which she and Mark lived. Both women continued comparing notes on the availability of local produce while they served the coffee and tea. John was standing at the deck railing, staring beyond the end of the garden.

"Mark. Who's your backyard neighbor?" he asked.

"I think it's someone in banking, a Mr. Kratz. We met him once or twice, some years ago."

"I love the view; it's so quiet."

"Theresa and I enjoy it all the more now that the children have left the nest."

As they enjoyed their coffee or tea they talked about getting together for another meal but did not set a definite date. The visitors thanked their hosts for a wonderful feast and a relaxing time and promised to keep in touch now that they had re-established contact. The hosts wished them a safe trip as John and Jean drove off.

As soon as they got to West Chester John remarked,

"What a catastrophe. Timothy seemed to have so much potential for good."

Ever so briefly, he recalled the pioneering work of Reverend e'Muthembwa, whose reputation had been besmirched by his founding of a new denomination. As told to John by other missionaries, the reverend had shortened his otherwise outstanding ministry because he was mule-headed and full of pride.

"We'll say a prayer for him tonight," said his wife.

Timothy Muthengi had kept little contact with his friend during the final months of his bible school training. E'Muthembwa heard second hand that the former deacon had completed his training but when he got his first posting they lost contact completely while each was busy nurturing his own congregation. The preacher was therefore surprised and disappointed when a disheveled Timothy showed up one Monday morning at the Kithongoto church, reeking of native beer and looking old beyond his years. He was in need of serious counseling, and without faltering, his old friend shepherded him through a long and at times tortured recovery. There were times during Timothy's five months of prayer and supervision by his mentor that the recovering alcoholic failed to show up or was too drunk to follow what was going on. At times, e'Muthembwa had to call on the local chief for help in making sure that Timothy could not easily find any local brew.

Almost as if he was cursed by his name, Timothy Muthengi neither recovered completely nor returned to his former denomination. He joined his mentor's congregation but he would occasionally disappear for days to re-appear red-eyed, disorientated and unable to explain where he had been. As he got older his drinking bouts decreased and in fact he remained sober long enough to become a church deacon again, before he suddenly died.

The day he chose to go 'wandering' there was a sudden and furious tropical thunderstorm. To keep from getting drenched by the heavy downpour he sought shelter under a huge African flame tree whose branches stretched almost the entire width of the path he was following. Just as he leaned on the tree trunk a bright light blinded his vision. For a brief moment, he thought he was finally seeing the Almighty. He did not hear the thunderclap that followed as lightning split the entire tree trunk open and almost simultaneously set it on fire.

A neighbor found his scorched body several meters away from where the tree had stood.

None could remember anyone being struck by lightning in the oral history of Kithongoto. The older and barely literate members of the church believed poor Timothy had tested his creator too many times until finally God got furious and ended the charade.

To the younger, educated generation in the church, his demise was no more than a chance accident which, through his ignorance, Timothy had helped by sheltering under the tallest tree in the wooded area. When these young, literate members tried to explain to the elders how lightning comes about, how his demise was likely happenstance rather than the willful act of the divine, they were silenced by being reminded that "the Lord works in mysterious ways" and they needed to mend their ways if they did not want to meet the same end.

By this time in the life of the congregation, most of the congregants over the age of twenty were educated beyond high school and many had modern, urban worldviews, having experienced city life.

Reverend e'Muthembwa was troubled by the divergence of opinion among his flock. All of these church members believed in an omnipotent, omnipresent and omniscient god; however, the older generation saw Him as manifesting retribution for lack of faith through nature while the younger viewed God as uninvolved in natural phenomena. "It must be an inter-generational gap, each reaching a different conclusion from the same event," thought the preacher. This caused him to question his own beliefs in the dogma of the church. Will the interpretation of such events matter when all of us are called to account for our actions on this earth?

In the end he decided what was more important was how he was going to heal the division between the old and the young in the congregation. He was able to deflect the conflict in their discussions by pointing out that as Christians they had more urgent obligations to fulfill on this earth than arguing over what God did or did not intend.

Personally he had not given thought to the force behind

131

his friend's death. He doubted that God had become angry with Timothy but he was certain that He had decided to call him home. The preacher did not indulge in such interpretations of the scriptures as expounded by the two groups. His view was of a god who is merciful and helpful, a benevolent deity. At Timothy's burial service Reverend e'Muthembwa was therefore clear in his conscience when he invoked the Almighty to keep the soul of his troubled friend in peace. "He has gone to his final resting place," the reverend said to the gathered crowd.

He was not sure where his friend had ended, heaven or hell. To the dismay of some in the congregation, Timothy Muthengi was given a proper burial in the church cemetery.

ELEVEN

E 'MUTHEMBWA LEARNT MUCH about his congregation through counseling for he was an excellent listener. Combining confidential information gathered during these sessions with public confessions during church services he was able to come up over the years with an approach that allowed him to be a better church leader.

At the funeral of Dr. Wambua Itumo, one of the sons of the church education committee chairman, the preacher struck up what initially appeared to him a customary conversation of solace with Dr. Nzungo Itumo, the younger brother of the deceased. He was a well-educated man who had done well for himself and was a staunch supporter of the educational program at the church. He had been very close to his deceased brother and to the reverend it appeared the younger man wanted to talk with his former pastor so e'Muthembwa, as usual, obliged.

The death of his elder brother had left the doctor overwrought. Unwilling and uncomfortable about talking to his own father about the loss of his closest brother he sought the ear of the pastor who invited him for a private one-on-one conversation in the church office. Between bouts of tears over his dead brother, repressed anger towards his father over his brutality early in Nzungo's life and his own siblings for not carrying their full adult weight the young man revealed the following story:

A few feet from the only outside door of the house where the family slept, the rhino whip hung, at hand when needed during the ploughing season. The rhinoceros hide, fashioned into a round handle with a long tapering section ending in a fine point, could produce a loud crackling sound if you flicked it or a stinging sensation on an ox's thick hide. When Kioko and Wambua, Nzungo's elder brothers, ploughed the family fields they used it to frighten the oxen. They never struck the oxen hard with it for fear of injuring the animals' skin, thus raising their father's ire. Tending the fields was a chore they did only during the weekends or on school holidays.

Their father was a strong advocate of education. He helped build the first neighborhood school with his own hands, cutting and hewing timber for the structure and its doors and windows. He had worked with others in the proverbial "raising of the barn" in order to ensure there was a place where all their children could go to learn the "the three Rs" (reading, writing and arithmetic.) Their father was so keen to send them to school that his children were always three or more years younger than their classmates. No child of his was going to remain uneducated because of idleness for he would rather draw and quarter the miscreant in the figurative sense. He believed strongly in the adage 'spare the rod and spoil the child.'

Late one afternoon, three-year-old Nzungo was playing near the kitchen hut with Kioko, his oldest brother. He looked forward to this time, having fun with either of his nine or six year-old brothers after they came home from school.

Suddenly, their father returned from the fields where he had been working with their mother. He determinedly marched into the larger building where they all slept and came out with the rhino whip in his hand. Holding the whip at the point where it started tapering from the handle, he briskly walked over to where Nzungo and his brother were playing. Like an automaton, he reached forward and grabbed the older boy's arm, and simultaneously struck him with the whip. The sound of the first strike was bone chilling. Nzungo could not understand why their loving and protective father had suddenly become this raging terror.

The first blow was immediately followed by a second and a third, each landing on the nearest part of his young body. By now Kioko was wailing. The fourth blow found the nine-year old in a fetal position, whimpering. Unheard, Nzungo was shouting at their father to stop. The strikes contin-

ued to rain, each with a full-grown man's force, leaving a six-inch long and half an inch deep cut where the whip landed. Nzungo's voice was getting hoarse. Soon his brother's bare calves and shins appeared to be wearing Roman sandal thongs, laced with a combination of white-gray and red as they crisscrossed.

All Nzungo could see was the rhino whip rise and fall with a determined regularity and wanton force on his older brother, now curled up into a ball and making tiny, feeble sounds like a dog ready to expire. It seemed to Nzungo that the more he shouted at his father the harder the blows fell, but he continued until he could shout no more. He could not save his brother from the savagery; he was helpless. Unable to alleviate the torture of his older brother and scared beyond his three-year-old wits, Nzungo had yelled and cried himself into a voiceless silence.

With the same suddenness it had started, without any warning, the whip stopped rising and falling. Their father walked away without a word. A few feet away from Nzungo lay the now all-bloodied and semi-comatose "remains" that was his older brother. The three-year-old had screamed and cried himself dry and could do no more than whisper. His voice was gone! He did not move away: frozen with fear, Nzungo stared vacantly at his silent brother.

It was still light and their mother had not yet returned from the fields. When she came back at dusk, neither child had moved, not even an inch.

Traumatized, Nzungo was still sitting at the same place he was before their father left and his brother, a motionless ball, lay where the whip had felled him. He was completely silent and the blood in his wounds had congealed.

Their mother took one look and immediately picked Nzungo's brother up. As she took him into the house she directed her middle son, Wambua, who had just returned from herding the family goats, to get the fire going and start heating some water. She told Nzungo to go into the kitchen and sit by the warm fire until she could get him something to eat. The three-year old pulled himself out of his trance-like state, quietly got up and slowly trudged into the kitchen.

When Wambua brought the warm water to their mother he found her quietly muttering to herself, "What kind of beast would do this to his own child?" He did not think that it was up to him to respond to a question whose answer required more than his six-year-old brain could muster. Besides, Wambua realized that his mother was just thinking aloud; she was not even looking at him so the question must not have been addressed to him.

From that night onward, their mother washed and treated her oldest child's wounds every morning and evening for the next three months. The chill between their parents as well as the violent incident affected the previous warmth between the children and their father. Nzungo was never sure what might set their father off on another insane rampage and no explanation

137

regarding the mauling of their brother by their father was given to the children. Everyone was tense as well as wary around the man of the house.

Unbeknownst to the children, the night following the brutal beating their parents had come to an understanding, that if ever such savagery occurred again their mother would leave with all the children and never come back. They had agreed that all future disciplining would be done together, thus guard against either losing their temper to the point of insanity while chastising the children.

Their father did not take this arrangement kindly because he resented being cornered by his wife. Over the years his displeasure developed into inaction with the consequence that whenever the children needed disciplining he deferred that responsibility to their mother. At times, according to Nzungo, he just did not seem to care. This default arrangement left the busy mother, with nine children to look after, with little time for the nurturing they needed. Such parental abdication denied the younger siblings the guidance they needed in order to do well either in school or later in their lives.

It was not until several years later when Nzungo started attending school that Wambua told him why their brother had been so savagely beaten: he had lied to his parents all those days when he was supposed to be in school. Their father had suddenly found out that Kioko used to leave the house at the same time Wambua did and

*return at about the same time, having spent the
whole time hanging out with his friends, engaging
in unwholesome and probably illegal activities.*

Reverend e'Muthembwa advocated strong discipline
but concluded that the head of the church education committee had misunderstood the precepts of Christianity in
raising his children. Being the diplomat that he was he did
not voice such an opinion to Nzungo. He counseled his
parishioner to forgive his father and brothers for any per-
ceived harm they may have done in the past and said,
"Nzungo, treasure those of your family who remain on earth
now that your beloved brother has passed on." After giving
the doctor a few minutes to regain his composure, he offered
his continued counsel whenever Nzungo felt the need for a
caring and willing ear and then they went out together to
face the rest of the mourners at the reception.

Dr. Itumo's experience made the preacher question his
own ability to convey the true meaning of Christian morals
to others but in the end; he realized he had no control over
how anyone else interpreted the scriptures. Listening to the
doctor's story, however, gave him pause to reflect on his
own parenting. "Had he been too harsh in disowning his
young first son?" he wondered.

That night he prayed the Lord to give him the wisdom
to communicate His love and mercy more effectively.

TWELVE

NZUNGO, THE THIRD child, never quite understood his elder brother, Kioko, who seemed bent on frustrating their parents' desire for them to be educated. His young mind had not fathomed the clash of wills between his eldest brother and their father. Nzungo decided early in his youth that Kioko's example would lead only to dashed dreams, ultimately many disappointments and probably additional beatings.

He eschewed his eldest brother's company, especially when he opted for ditching school, and instead sought out Wambua, who was, according to their parents, headed for great things. Wambua had become the model that Nzungo followed, always looking up to him, ready to equal if not excel him. Not only was Wambua a studious youngster but he shunned sloth as he attacked every assigned chore with gusto and would not pause until it was completed. This attitude always kept him in the good graces of their strict and controlling father, a fact that made an early impression on his young brother. "There will be no rhino whip for me," Nzungo had said to himself.

As Wambua and Nzungo got older they behaved like twins: they would do chores together, study together and when it came to passing messages to their first-crush girl-friends, be emissaries for each other. Each was determined not to let the other down as they went through their teen years and into college, each pushed by the other and their parents' exhortations. Each tried to outdo the other in a brotherly competition for good grades even though they were never in the same class. If one did poorly, the other felt equally bad. Whenever life's demands seemed unbearable the brothers would remind each other, "Remember the rhino whip." Their fear became their rallying cry.

Years later Nzungo and Wambua realized the whipping incident had left an indelible mark on their approach to life. Even though neither of them acknowledged it, their father's brutality had left them with lasting emotional scars, which made the two brothers lean ever so heavily on each other in order get any sense of security. Fear of such harsh treatment became the impetus that drove them to work diligently at their studies and in their careers. By then the family had grown to include six brothers and three sisters, all two or three years apart in age. Fortunately, the younger siblings knew nothing about the rhino whip. To Nzungo it seemed their father either had mellowed or was afraid his entire family would desert him if he exercised his earlier brutality towards the children.

The bond between the two brothers was so strong that the other children often felt left out when Wambua and Nzungo got together. The alienation was especially acute when, as high school youngsters, the two chose to practice their newly acquired linguistic skill by conversing in the English language, which the others barely understood.

In later years, the break from their brothers and sisters was exacerbated by the fact that the two were the only college graduates among the nine children. Indeed, very few of their peers in the whole eastern part of the district had ever seen the inside of a college campus and the community could easily count the number of the literate amongst them. At the time only four other people in the location had tenth grade education.

In essence, Wambua and Nzungo often found themselves in a unique situation, one in which they could discuss many of their problems only with each other. Ideas about what the future might hold for a university-educated person remained hard to imagine. No one could inform them, but they shared their father's belief in the benefits of being well educated. With this firm belief, they pursued their studies.

Although their interests led them into different areas of specialization, in the end both chose the same profession, medicine, and even practiced in the same hospital during the early years in their careers. Even though they attended different universities they were truly never apart. As their careers advanced, geographical distance or even busy schedules could not diminish the affection they had for each other.

As each raised his own family, they would often share wisdom on how to undertake parenthood successfully. They would also talk about how the rest of their younger brothers and sisters had squandered their chances in spite of the help and guidance Wambua and Nzungo had offered to each one.

Despite their frustrations, the two brothers continued to

lend a helping hand to the struggling and often idle brothers and sisters. To help support their younger siblings as well as take care of their aging parents, they set up a trust fund to which they generously contributed every month. It was supposed to be accessed only by their father, not by any of the extended family.

Throughout their adult life, the one who lived closer to the family homestead would be the conduit for the other for information about their larger family. As their jobs moved them from one hospital to another, the role of keeping connected with the rest of the family moved back and forth. News about the family was often mundane, who was doing what or had gone where, but every once in while things would heat up.

Late one night Nzungo picked up the ringing telephone. An exasperated Wambua came on,

"Hello! Sorry, I have not had a chance to return your call." They knew each other's voices so well that neither ever bothered to identify himself on the telephone.

"You could've written," Nzungo teased.

"Nothing serious to report. The parents are doing well, if only our brothers would let them be."

Nzungo could sense an edge in Wambua's voice. Something was amiss.

"Oh. What are they up to now?" Nzungo inquired.

"You remember some time ago Kioko attempted to embezzle from the trust? It seems this time he has succeeded. There's hardly enough for our parents to cover this month's expenses!"

"Can we sue him?" Nzungo interjected.

"I'm sure we could. The trouble is, if we did and he surely ought to be convicted, we will then be stuck with supporting his family of eight kids as well as our parents."

"You've a point there. Did you get a chance to ask him what he did with the money?"

"Yes. Apparently, he got involved in a worthless business deal and lost all the money he stole." Wambua explained.

"I wish I could believe him! I wonder how he managed to bypass the precautions we set up. Perhaps someone at the bank was in cahoots with him?"

"I didn't bother to ask. According to the branch manager, Kioko presented a check, duly signed by father, for half of the funds in the trust. Anyway, I changed the set-up. From now on either you or I will cash all the checks. Somehow or other we'll have to visit Dad and Mum more often. It seems this is the only way we can make sure they get the money."

"That's no guarantee. They've had cash stolen from the house on several occasions. There's no foolproof way of making sure the money is judiciously spent. We *could* buy everything for them, but that would be impractical. Besides, those leeches would not hesitate to take whatever they wanted from Dad and Mum," Nzungo said bitterly.

"That's exactly my thinking," Wambua added. "Anyway, let's try this new set-up and hope it works."

"I hope it does. Well, take care of yourself and give my love to Mwelu and the girls," Nzungo concluded.

"Hello to Kaindi and the boys," Wambua said as he hung up.

As the years went by it became obvious to Wambua and Nzungo that their ne'er-do-well brothers always treated whatever the two brothers owned as their own property, free to dispose of anyway they saw fit. Even though they never contributed to the trust fund, they believed they had equal say in the disposal of any money directed towards their parents' welfare. As if that was not infuriating enough, the siblings would misappropriate supplies and furnishings intended for the comfort of the aging parents – often with the excuse that their own large families needed help too. They knew how to have broods of children but not how to take care of them.

Every time they showed up at either Wambua's or Nzungo's house, for the all-too-frequent and unannounced visits, which was in keeping with African tradition, it was a cat and mouse game. They would try to abscond with as much of material goods as they could lay their long sticky fingers on, while Wambua or Nzungo tried to keep them away from anything the siblings might find tempting. Anything, anywhere, including closets in the house, was fair game. One literally had to count the silverware before the brothers departed from the house! Unfortunately, Wambua and Nzungo did not always succeed in keeping track of everything.

Such was the case with Wambua's formal shoes. As he got dressed for a formal black-tie affair - black and white tuxedo, black socks – he could not find his imported, black, patent leather shoes. He accused his wife of misplacing them while he settled for the only other half-decent pair he owned – medium brown, six-eyelet oxfords. He was embarrassed to appear in his official capacity as the Ministry of Health's envoy for the World Health Organization conference. Months later, when one of his brothers showed up for another unannounced visit, Wambua saw his now scuffed and stretched black shoes on his brother's feet. He was fit to be tied.

"Tell me. Are those my shoes?" he demanded.

"H-u-u-h. Yes," his younger sibling feebly answered. Then he found his verbal stride and continued, "The last time I was here I noticed that when you dressed for work you did not wear this pair. I needed shoes and knew you would not give me money to buy any. Therefore, I took these. I knew you wouldn't mind."

"Wouldn't mind!" Wambua shouted. "Didn't you ever think of asking if it was OK to take them? Besides, how can you support your own family when you can't even buy your own shoes?" he asked sarcastically. Half-way turning towards his wife, Wambua continued, "From now on, you are not welcome in this house. Tomorrow morning I expect you to leave my home. I will give you a one-way bus fare but no more. Are we clear?"

The younger brother remained silent, his face assuming the expression of one whose feelings are hurt. He looked crushed. The following morning when Wambua handed him the bus fare there was neither an apology nor expression of gratitude; the younger man simply took the money and headed out to the bus stop without saying goodbye to anyone, in every sense playing the aggrieved party.

Such shenanigans only cemented the already close relationship between the two brothers because each knew the other suffered almost identical trials and therefore could relate to the suffering caused by their own siblings. As adults they had grown to be so much alike that casual acquaintances often mistook one for the other; even the way they spoke was uncannily similar. No one knows whether this was so because of their shared experiences or just genetics but when Wambua suddenly died, Nzungo - half-way round the world - knew at the same moment it happened.

"Don't feel bad for me. I'm ready to go," Wambua told him in a dream.

THIRTEEN

R EVEREND E'MUTHEMBWA WAS successful in converting people in the Kithongoto community to Christianity but found many hesitant when he told them they had to abandon the custom of paying bride price for their sons' brides. This traditional way of augmenting the family wealth was indeed difficult to pry from the conscience of the recently converted believers. It was especially troublesome when poor parents had sacrificed so much to educate their daughters in order to ensure a higher bride price. Society saw female children as having no other value in the families in which they were born. Therefore, how could he convince parents to spend money on their daughters and then simply give them away?

The reverend was not wealthy by any means; he had no cattle or goats. So he thought if he led by example perhaps he would convince the diehards. While his oldest daughter, Ndoti, was growing up and going through her nurse's training, e'Muthembwa chose not to take to task those who demanded bride price for the marriage of their daughters. He knew that soon enough it would be his turn to show them that a true Christian does not ask bride price for one's daughter. Then he would push those who insisted on asking for bride price to make a choice between Christianity and traditional beliefs. When that time came he lost a few families but many more stayed in the church.

Within a span of four years Esther Ndoti completed her training and was hired as a senior nurse in a hospital in Nairobi. This development in her career would lead to a fortuitous meeting with Nyamai at a church they both attended.

Several years ago Nyamai had been the first from his area to graduate from college. In fact, he had been a trendsetter when he was among the first group of students to enroll at the newly established high school in his district, sixty or so miles from his home. Shortly after graduating with a degree in engineering he got a job with a firm headquartered in the capital city of Nairobi. The first month was hectic because Nyamai had to find a flat to rent and generally learn to take care of his new home. His years in college had taught him nothing about this since all his living needs had been catered for by the university through his scholarship.

In a city where rentals ranged from brick-walled estates with guards armed with AK47s to tin-roof shacks in the slums, Nyamai had a difficult time finding just the right place. With the frequent muggings and general insecurity in all parts of the city, he was concerned about his own safety but his income limited his search for a flat.

City life was challenging but he was determined to make a go of it. Towards the end of his first month of work, Nyamai found a vacancy in a three storey, reinforced concrete building in one of the recent, hastily constructed residential developments at the edge of town, next to one of the oldest shantytowns in the city. A single road led to the development. At the entrance, a small, concrete structure sheltered an armed guard. Armed, that is, if one considers a wooden club and small, hunting knife adequate weapons for protecting the poorly fenced-off buildings. The six identical buildings had no elevators. They reminded one of cheap motels, each built around its own poorly maintained inner courtyard with sparsely planted, hastily pruned, yellowing bougainvillea.

The echo of one's footsteps could be heard along the entire wing of the building as one moved up the uncarpeted stairs or along the bare hallway. The structure vibrated with every footfall, threatening to buckle under one's weight but remained standing. Entering Nyamai's long, rectangular single-bedroom flat one immediately noticed the cheap furniture and the bare concrete floor with equally bare windows, the only exception being the medium-sized window in the back wall of the bedroom. A tightly stretched cloth held in place by a thin wire attached to the wall with nails covered this window, blocking the view of slum dwellings a few yards over the property fence.

The flat was so small that only one person could manage to live in it. It had a combination sitting/dining area next to a cubicle of an electric kitchen. With the exception of the stuffed easy chair that Nyamai had bought secondhand shortly after he moved in, the two crudely made wooden chairs, a small table and a two-shelf metal bookcase next to the outside door made up the original furniture. For some time, he'd had plans to buy better furniture and redecorate but at the end of each month he found himself short of funds for such extravagance.

The truth was he never knew how much money he was likely to have at the end of each month. He earned enough to support two adults in the city and have some left over for future needs but the problem was that he found it difficult to turn away the less fortunate who came visiting from his home community. Relatives, neighbors and friends of friends from his area all descended on him every time they visited the city. They showed up unexpectedly, ready to be welcomed; they brought nothing but expected everything – all the comforts of home. In fact, they rarely lifted a finger to help, claiming ignorance about how to fend for themselves around Nyamai's flat.

Every time they came to visit, Nyamai had to literally step over somebody to get to the kitchen or go out. When more than two were asleep on the floor at night, he had to take off his shoes and use his toes to feel his way around the flat to avoid injuring someone.

The steady and unexpected visits became a damper on his lifestyle and a drain on his finances. It was not enough that Nyamai generously hosted all who invaded his flat, moreover, relatives always expected a "little extra something" before their departure. Sometimes the situation was so grim that it could make an adult cry. However, as a selfless but impractical Christian, he managed to survive the onslaught.

Holidays were especially difficult for him, Christmas being the worst. The amount of money he could spend on presents depended on whether he'd had recent visitors, some of whom had a knack for showing up near the end of each month – the time when Nyamai was paid.

Regardless of whether it was Christmas time or any other holiday, everyone around his hometown expected the local star, the one with the big city job, to come home with something for everyone! It was the lord of the manor visiting the serfs' cottages, bestowing favors on each household. His own parents were no different in this respect; they measured their son's status by the number and type of presents he brought for his large immediate family and several times as many near relatives.

No explanation would suffice for coming home with less or nothing at all, even for those who had visited him less than a month earlier. How could he claim to be poor when he lived like rich city people? He had electricity, running water (some of it was even pumped in hot) and he did not even use firewood like ordinary people. It was impossible to reconcile the finite and the infinite, a cultural gap spanning nearly a century of changes. What was essential to one was a luxury to the other: a life of individual self-sufficiency in which one bought everything was alien to a society centered on communal survival.

When Nyamai started working he used to visit his relatives at least once every month. Soon he realized he could not afford to lavish everyone with presents every time he visited. The guilt started piling up, gnawing at his conscience. He could neither escape nor face the relentless accusations of being a tightwad. No one sympathized with his dilemma as no one understood that he had a limited budget, that every aspect of his life in the city required him to spend money.

To escape the torture, Nyamai cut back on his home visits, traveling to see his relatives once every three months. The change did not bring the intended financial relief; instead, it increased the number of impromptu visits by others from his village.

That is when he decided to try a different strategy, to spend as little time at his flat as possible. They still came and if he was not home they sat and waited outside his building, courtesy of the gatekeeper. There was no way of avoiding them unless he started sleeping somewhere else! Some of his flat neighbors even accused him of being too harsh on his relatives, friends and acquaintances.

His new strategy did not significantly reduce the amount of money he doled out to the unexpected visitors. Therefore, he decided he could only afford to visit his home once a year, at which point his parents started complaining. Nyamai invited them to visit him but they declined, telling him the city was too far for them to travel and his flat too small. They did not know how much their son yearned for more spacious accommodations. Despite the annual increments in his salary and his frugal lifestyle, Nyamai was unable to save enough to afford a flat with more than one bedroom.

In the intervening period, Nyamai had become active in a church in the city. While attending one of its functions, he had met Ndoti Muthembwa, a supervising nurse at one of the Nairobi hospitals. The vivacious young woman had impressed Nyamai with her wit and sense of self. Although he had not been planning to get married anytime soon, he found himself thinking of the nurse he had met. The next time he saw Ndoti he made sure that he left with her telephone number in his pocket and within a short time they were going out on a regular basis.

Some months after they became acquainted, Nyamai began to realize he needed to make major changes in his relationship with his hometown community if he was going to get better acquainted with this charming, intelligent woman. He was thrilled to be dining out and going to movies with Ndoti but every shilling he spent left him feeling guilty. That Ndoti was a well-paid supervising nurse at one of the leading private hospitals in the city and often paid her own way did not lessen Nyamai's feelings of guilt. He did not want to disappoint her for he had begun to care too much to give her a reason to think less of him.

One day Ndoti had to leave town to visit her parents and was delayed; she did not return at the time she said she would. Nyamai found himself calling her flat every half hour, hoping she would pick up the telephone. By three o'clock in the morning he was beside himself with worry. Ndoti had taken one of the rickety, smoke belching country minibuses which are small trucks converted to carry fourteen passengers and are famous for their drivers' recklessness. Minibuses accounted for more than their share of traffic accidents as the brightly decorated contraptions sped reck-lessly along the poorly maintained country dirt roads, their sole goal being to be the first among their competitors to get to the next stop.

Oftentimes, accidents went unreported for more than a day because of the absence of telephones and the perennial inefficiency of the traffic police. This made Nyamai's appre-hension all the more acute. Ndoti could at that moment be lying at the bottom of some forsaken ditch in need of aid she was never going to get. He had difficulty falling asleep since he was convinced that Ndoti had been in one of the all too frequent mishaps. He became fully aware of how much she had become a part of his life and that he could not imagine going on without her.

He dearly loved her.

At breakfast all he could stomach was a cup of coffee with lots of milk; he had no appetite. He anxiously listened to the morning news on the radio but here was no mention of any minibus accident on the previous day. He willed himself to go to work but when he got there he could not keep his attention focused on the project he needed to complete by the end of that day. His thoughts were taken up by worries about Ndoti.

Nyamai did not go out for lunch but instead chose to stay in the office, hoping to catch the mid-day newscast. When the one o'clock news came on there was no mention of any accident, nothing there to alleviate his fears or lessen his apprehension. He made himself a cup of instant coffee with real cream and sat sipping as he stared at the window. His co-workers were trickling back from lunch, he noticed. Just then the telephone at his desk rang and as usual he expected the receptionist to answer it. Before he realized that it could be someone calling with news of Ndoti, the ringing stopped.

As if it was catching its breath, the telephone started ringing again. He almost jumped as he reached for the hand-set,

"Hello. Mutumbi Engineers, Nyamai speaking."

"I was afraid you'd be out for lunch," a familiar but harassed voice greeted his ear. "I'm sorry I didn't return yesterday. I'll explain when I see you this evening. I hope you weren't too worried. I was late so I came to work straight from the bus stop. It's chaotic here. We'll talk later. Bye."

She hung up before he could even tell her he was glad

she was safe. There was so much he wanted to tell her right at that moment but it had to wait. A heavy weight had been lifted off his shoulders; he could breathe again. All he had to do was bridge the time between then and that evening. He had never been a clock-watcher but that afternoon Nyamai was counting the minutes until eight when he knew Ndoti would get away from work.

When they met after work they talked long into the night, starting with how Ndoti had missed the last minibus from her village. They bemoaned the absence of telephones in the rural areas and the state of public transportation beyond the city limits. They shared their worries about each other and how they hated being apart. By the end of the evening they were talking marriage.

This was the happiest Nyamai had been in a long time; he was euphoric. As the full meaning of their engagement dawned on him, Nyamai became even more determined to make changes in his financial priorities: he had to stop, once and for all, the stream of people who descended on his flat seeking free boarding; he had to resolve the issue of presents to the whole neighborhood. He had to start thinking of the family he and Ndoti were planning to have not too far in the future.

First he had to find a larger flat, away from where he was now living. He and his fiancée were planning to get married within the year. By the end of three months, Nyamai had moved into a two bedroom flat, situated on the second floor in a two-storey building about a mile from his work, in an area that discouraged loitering. The building had a front door guarded by a burly ex-soldier armed with an automatic pistol. He allowed no one beyond the front door other than residents; guests had to be met there by their hosts.

The flat came unfurnished, thus giving Nyamai and Ndoti the opportunity to entertain their whims in making the place livable. By combining their earnings they were able to afford, in addition to the furniture, a maroon wool rug, around which they arranged the sitting room pieces. Nyamai told no one in his home community that he had moved; he was, to some extent, hiding.

For fear of upsetting her parents Ndoti did not mention that she was moving in with her fiancé. She thought the puritanical preacher would probably have skinned her alive or disowned her. It was fortunate for her that her parents were not in the habit of visiting their working daughter in the city.

The following Christmas, Nyamai did not go to visit his parents but instead, he sent them presents. He chose to spend the holidays in the city with Ndoti, making only a two-day trip over Christmas to meet her parents at Kithongoto.

When they arrived her mother was the only one at home. She was delighted that her daughter chose to spend the holiday with them and she was dying to find out more about the young man who accompanied her. She invited them to sit down while they waited for her father to return from visiting a housebound congregant. After a half-hour of small chitchat Kanini was getting impatient and started the questions before her husband returned.

"Did you already get married without telling us?" she inquired.

"Why would I want to deny papa the pleasure of marrying me off?" Ndoti countered with a radiant smile on her face. "We're engaged and hope papa will do the honors."

The preacher walked in as Ndoti was talking about the engagement. He was not sure he understood the gist of the conversation, having grown up in a culture in which young women did not negotiate or decide who they were going to marry. He wondered whether this was the new world of educated women that he would have to get used to. One consequence he didn't like about educating girls was that they talked and thought too much. He remembered that it was not too long ago that their second child, Joseph Mutunga, had blind-sided them by marrying outside the race without first consulting them. What was the world coming to?

"And who are you going to marry?" he asked as he put his hat on a hook in the wall near the front door.

Nyamai had stood to greet the preacher when he came in but e'Muthembwa did not notice the young man immediately.

"No greetings, papa?" Ndoti asked playfully. He lightly placed his hand over his daughter's head and said,

"Welcome home, child."

"Papa, meet Nyamai, the man I'm engaged to marry," Ndoti said sheepishly and without making eye contact. She kept her head down in the traditional attitude of respect for elders.

"What do we know about him? Can he support you?" her father asked brusquely.

The introduction had not gone well at all. The old man was less courteous than Ndoti had anticipated and the questions were coming faster than she could handle. "Had she miscalculated what her parents' reaction was going to be?" she thought as panic set in.

Unsure of what her next action should be, confront, flee, or stay and be quiet, she looked at her fiancé for support. Without comment Nyamai sat down again, his gaze directed towards the tightly clasped hands on his lap, ready for the next salvo.

No sooner was he seated than the preacher started peppering him with questions: where was he born, who were his parents, what church did he attend, what kind of work did he do?

"Papa! You're treating him like a criminal," Ndoti protested, trying to keep her voice down in a respectful manner but feeling very upset.

"That's alright. They have a right to know," Nyamai calmly interjected.

"Well, that's true, if you're going to be part of this family we should know all about you," her mother said softly, trying to save the situation from deteriorating into a clash between father and daughter.

E'Muthembwa did not take kindly to being interrupted by his daughter but he stopped interrogating Nyamai. The young man went on to allay their apprehension by offering to answer whatever questions the parents might have about him.

The preacher was proud that his daughter had found a bright and suitable future husband but dared not bring up the topic of negotiating with Nyamai's parents, having learnt something about modern views when his son married Sue Gilchrist. Traditionally, it was the responsibility of the groom's family to initiate the process.

That night Ndoti and Nyamai slept in separate bedrooms, relieved her father had not gotten into a snit and thrown both of them out. After the initial skirmish everything had settled down. Now happy, they looked forward to getting away so they could be themselves again. They were both pleased and surprised that her father did not talk of bride price. What they didn't know was that after preaching against it he would not have dared. Besides, how would he have explained to the congregation the sudden appearance of cows and goats at his homestead? They might wonder, nonetheless, if he was waiting to ask for the equivalent in hard cash.

Their subsequent visits to her parents' home were more amiable as her father seemed to take a liking to Nyamai. The two got on wonderfully well as they talked about what her future husband called "man things." Ndoti had never seen her father so happy and proud as when he married them at the African Brotherhood Church at Kithongoto. Nyamai and his family had paid for the wedding expenses but there was never any demand for bride price: the preacher had stuck to his guns.

Nyamai had decided early in his relationship with Ndoti to wean himself from feeling obligated to play Santa Claus all year long. As a grateful and responsible son he sent money to his parents every month but from that time on, he saw his parents on only a few occasions: at his and Ndoti's wedding, after the birth of their son and when his mother came to the city for medical attention. He could neither afford the expense nor bear the hassle of having to lavish his nonexistent riches on the whole of his old neighborhood.

His parents missed him but were still proud of this son who had not only landed a good job in the city, but with no help from them had managed to marry a woman from a respectable family in his own tribe who was educated and a nurse, to boot! They ignored the occasional and indirect snide remarks about his stinginess. They vaguely understood what he had explained to them about this being the modern way of life and hoped he was right that whatever they lost now in village status would be regained when the money saved would be put toward the education of their grandson and they would see him graduate from university.

Who could know what grand things their grandson and future grandchildren might accomplish?

FOURTEEN

R EVEREND GIDEON E'MUTHEMBWA lived and preached at
Kithongoto for over thirty years before he handed
over the vibrant congregation to one of his early
converts. He continued to participate in church activities and
infrequently gave the Sunday sermon. His old body was
tired, his sight was failing and he had stopped tilling the land
years before. Mutunga, his second child, was now paying the
lion's share of his parents' living expenses.

The old preacher knew his son worked for some organization with offices in Nairobi but he did not know exactly
what Mutunga did. All that mattered to him was that the rest
of his children had done well in school and seemed to be
secure in their careers. He was happy and content to play the
doting grandfather while he 'waited for the Lord to call him
home.'

My full name is Joseph Mutunga Muthembwa and I face

a dilemma. I'm in my early forties and second in command in a non-governmental organization (NGO) which is dedicated to improving the welfare of the disadvantaged in Kenya. I should mention that in this country as of recent times the word "president" refers to only one person in the entire nation – the political head of the Republic of Kenya. All other former presidents and vice presidents are now referred to as chairmen or vice chairmen. I used to be called the vice president, but not anymore.

If this had been the only change I would not mind but lately I have learnt that I need to belong to the right tribe and know just the right people in order to be promoted. Unfortunately, I neither belong to the right tribe nor intimately know the right political honchos. My salary is not predicated on my performance on the job but on my ranking in the NGO's hierarchical chart so it is most important that I retain at least my current position.

Ours is a country with a small circle of movers and shakers, the well-educated elite. Everyone in this power circle knows some aspect concerning the rest in the country. Sometimes I yearn for anonymity, to disappear from public view and continue doing my work. Such thoughts are mere pipe dreams, a wish for an impossible outcome in this small segment of society.

According to the powers that be I married into the wrong tribe too, the non-tribe of those foreigners. My spouse, Sue, happens to be foreign born and of the wrong color to boot! She is of European extraction and our children are derisively called half-caste: those without ethnicity, the un-grounded and unaffiliated with any tribe or race, neither black nor white. Tribe is paramount here; without it you are nothing in this society.

Sometimes this attitude makes me feel like doing serious harm to those who propagate such drivel, but I know better than to pick a fight with someone over ethnic slurs. With my dearth of political connections I would be sealing my doom. I wish it were a case of joining them or fighting them; but I find the former unacceptable and the latter guarantees my annihilation.

You might ask, "What brought this on? Why am I suddenly so disgruntled?" After all, I have been with this organization since its inception sixteen years ago. I was happy, content to be part of its management cadre until recently, when I learnt, almost by accident, that our ageing chairman was planning to retire within the next four months. I had been the deputy for this unassuming, mild mannered gentleman, his understudy, for nearly five years and never once did he express any concern or dissatisfaction with my job performance. On many occasions he had trusted me to represent the NGO in pivotal and delicate negotiations and had effusively complimented my acumen in articulating the goals of the organization to foreign donor governments. Yet, if my information is correct, the chairman has indicated that he would prefer to be replaced by someone from the correct tribe – his. *Should I bide my time and wait to see what happens or should I confront him about his two-faced behavior?* I wonder. Neither is a situation I want to face because neither is likely to produce an outcome I could stomach.

It has now been two months since I learnt of the chairman's impendent retirement and it seems to me I have a third choice. Or would it be cutting off my nose to spite my face? I could resign from the NGO and offer my services elsewhere, but by virtue of my present position I have achieved a level of notoriety which gives the inner circle of power the opportunity to frustrate any efforts I might make towards getting another position.

Looking for less financially rewarding jobs away from the seat of power would be a choice if it were not so detrimental to the welfare of my children. Besides, if I were to leave my present position would my family emerge unscathed after the resultant adjustments in our standard of living or would the change tear us apart? How would my ageing parents deal with their bread and butter siphon being tightened? In our culture children take care of the financial needs of parents since there is no social security or old age pension.

In any case, even if there were, my parents never worked outside their home. Theirs has always been purely subsistence living, a hand to mouth tilling of the family limited acreage. My father's work with the church had no provision for retirement benefits and in fact, when he was preaching, he was lucky if he got paid at all; it was always a hit and miss situation for preachers to get paid.

None of my choices is palatable but I must make one if I am to retain my sanity under the present circumstances. I am unwilling to accept the "usual way of doing things." I am more than that and if the authorities do not recognize my full worth then I will have no choice but to jump ship. I have shared my conundrum with my wife and although she appreciates my dilemma she would rather I did not stick my neck out, take such drastic action as resigning. Therefore, I bide my time.

At the retirement party for our departing chairman, his replacement was introduced. He is a medium-set, preening peacock of a man a few years younger than I am and about my height, five feet nine inches. It was immediately obvious that he is a man of dubious formal qualifications and matching ineptitude in dealing with personnel. I cannot see how he is going to lead an organization with over two hundred employees in the central office and almost as many out in the field.

His five-minute comments left several of us groaning inwardly, wondering why in the world the board ever gave him the job: he seemed to know nothing about the goals of the organization, his jokes were flat and his ability to communicate pathetic with his oft mispronounced words in English. It is doubtful he ever completed his college studies and if he did he learnt very little.

Rumor has it that our new chairman is the nephew of some bigwig politician, in addition to being distantly related to the retired man he has replaced. His total administrative experience spans a period of six months working as a bank manager in a small upcountry branch. I was incredulous when he admitted to knowing next to nothing about his new responsibilities while he expressed the hope that I would be generous with my knowledge and experience. No wonder the position was filled without the usual advertising, as is normal for such a pivotal job. I got the impression that I am expected to be doing all the heavy lifting while he reaps the praise, a situation I would find marginally tolerable provided he did not meddle with the NGO's revenues by siphoning off public funds for his own aggrandizement.

Towards the end of the new chairman's first week on the job he called a meeting with departmental heads on the following Wednesday morning. When I asked him for the meeting agenda this novice administrator gave me a blank stare until I asked in mild exasperation,

"What is the meeting going to be about?"

"Oh, I just want to know who the department heads are," he replied casually.

"Then we can meet briefly during the morning tea break," I suggested helpfully.

"No, I want a full meeting in the conference room. Would you make sure we have refreshments."

Getting refreshments was hardly an executive responsibility, so I bit my tongue and pointed out,

"Your secretary actually organizes refreshments. I'll alert her."

"OK. I'm going out for lunch and should be back by two."

With that statement he turned and headed for the elevator even though it was just after 10:30 a.m. I wondered whether his secretary knew where the new chairman had gone. His office is next to mine so I stopped at his secretary's desk to inquire whether she knew where the boss had gone.

A blank expression greeted my question and I almost broke out laughing when the telephone rang and the secretary replied,

"No, he's not in at the moment. ... He's is in meeting. Can I take a message?"

After the telephone call, I asked her whether she had the agenda for the Wednesday meeting and I got another blank stare. So I patiently explained that the chairman wanted to meet with all the departmental heads in the conference room the following Wednesday morning and as usual, the secretary was expected to arrange for refreshments.

"Thanks for letting me know," she said as I turned to go to my office. "I'll get the agenda when he comes back," she added.

"Good luck," I said over my shoulder, halfway to my office.

Half an hour before the end of the workday the secretary appeared at my office, all flustered. The meeting was scheduled for the following week and she did not even know at what time in the morning it was supposed to start. She had found no notes about the agenda on the chairman's desk and he had not returned from lunch. She reminded me that it was Friday and departmental heads normally needed three working days to prepare for such meetings.

Ms. Kalei has been the chairman's secretary for seven years. She's as precise as the proverbial Swiss clock, a woman whose sweet disposition belies an efficiency and business sense many executives would give anything to have.

"Welcome to the new way of doing business. Those who can, will, and as for the rest...," I cryptically observed. "Don't let it ruin your weekend, Ms. Kalei. The boss will sort it out when he comes in on Monday."

By Tuesday afternoon, however, I had not seen nor talked to the chairman since before lunch the previous Friday. Since Monday when those expected to attend the Wednesday meeting started asking, I had to field questions about a meeting of which I knew nothing. I sensed frustration, indeed exasperation, in their voices.

In truth, all are hardworking employees who hate wasting time over inconsequential meetings: they are used to preparing for sessions during which their work is scrutinized and substantive questions raised. They have no time for meetings in which nothing concrete is discussed. I apologized to all who asked for being equally clueless but did not go the next step and blame the new chairman for the mess.

169

Who knows, he might already have informers amongst this cadre.

On Wednesday morning the chairman came to work two hours late. I know because I ran into him at the elevator door after quizzing his secretary as to his whereabouts. That was the first time I had seen him that week.

"Are you ready for the meeting?" he inquired.

"What time are we meeting?" I asked.

"Is ten thirty a good time?"

"As good as any," I answered, even though I was aware that was less than thirty minutes away. "You might want to tell your secretary to notify the departmental heads," I added as I disappeared into the elevator. I was curious to see how he would pull it off.

There are four departments: accounting, grants administration, projects management and public relations. Even though all four departmental heads knew about the proposed meeting two of them had assumed it was postponed since they had not received the customary copy of the agenda. Instead, they had scheduled their commitments for the day accordingly and therefore were out of their offices that morning.

As soon as I returned to my office the chairman called me in.

"Did you inform all the departments about the meeting?" he inquired.

"Yes, I did. However, I need to reiterate that's not really my role. All you need to do is tell Ms. Kalei, your secretary, and she won't disappoint you," I replied with an edge to my voice.

My explanation seemed to irritate him but I stood my ground and stared back at him. After a few seconds I asked,

"Was that it?"

"Yes," he replied dismissively with a wave of his hand.

"Then I'll see you in the conference room in fifteen minutes," I said as I walked out of his office, asking myself why he still thought I was hired to run and fetch for him. Ten minutes later I made my way to the conference room where I found the accounting and grants administration departments were represented. The other two were not.

"Anybody know where Mwea and Kiplagat are?" I inquired of those present.

"Mwea went to check on the Mwabata project," the head of grants replied.

"And Kiplagat is supervising the medical clinic public announcement production at Mega Studios," the accounting head filled in.

I wondered why these two heads even showed up; my sentiments were with those who were out doing what they were hired to do. To tell the truth, I do not trust the grants administrator, so I said nothing as the three of us opted to enjoy a cup of tea while we waited for the chairman to show up. At a quarter to eleven he appeared, all self-important in his recently imported, chalk-striped navy-blue suit over a light blue, wide-collar shirt with a red power tie and a matching pocket kerchief. He strutted into the wood paneled room without a single piece of paper or his secretary to take minutes. He made a beeline for the tea table at the side, halfway down the room, without saying a single word to anyone or apologizing for being late. We waited silently, each absorbed in his thoughts.

When the chairman sat down at the head of the long, ovoid mahogany table the three of us flanked him on either side, the two departmental heads on one side and I on the other. An awkward minute or two passed before I decided we had sat idle long enough. Looking at the chairman I started,

"You've met Mr. Githiru and Mr. Kisigo, I believe. Messrs. Kiplagat and Mwea are out supervising departmental projects." I was aware of the fact that he had been introduced to the four gentlemen at the previous chairman's retirement party.

He ignored me and continued sipping his tea as if I had not spoken. His boorish behavior was beginning to get to me; as he failed to acknowledge the presence of either man I wondered how much of the preening novice we were expected to take. When he looked at me the chairman met my cold stare and demanded,

"Did you tell them this was an important meeting?" His tone was calculated to be confrontational, to establish once and for all that he was the top dog. It would have been comical if it were not being played by someone with so much responsibility resting on his inexperienced shoulders.

"You gave no agenda for this meeting. How could anyone know it was important?" I pointed out without raising my voice but ready to battle it out. All the slights he had given me during the past week and a half came to the fore in my retorts.

"I see. In that case the meeting is postponed until next week. *You* will prepare the agenda," he ordered. He gulped the last mouthful of tea and put his hands on the arms of his chair in order to get up.

"Not yet!" I interrupted.

My outburst caught him off guard and he remained seated, a boiler ready to explode.

"When I asked you about today's agenda you told me you wanted to meet the departmental heads. You've not even acknowledged the two who are present." I was on a roll. "You call the meeting, you furnish the agenda. Your secretary will prepare and distribute it for the meeting. That's *her* job."

As our confrontation escalated I could sense Messrs. Githiru and Kisigo were quite uncomfortable and would rather have been elsewhere. They remained fixed in their seats, each studying either his manicure or the lukewarm tea remaining in his cup. Perhaps they were afraid of being caught in the crossfire.

"Are you telling me what to do?" the chairman challenged.

"Not in so many words, but I believe if a person sees the need to call a meeting then the onus is on that person to give the ideas for such a meeting."

"You do what *I tell* you to do," he declared in a tone one uses to address a misbehaving child.

The thought of punching him crossed my mind but I recognized that such action would heap all the blame on me, so I banished it just as quickly and countered,

"Not according to my contract."

"We'll see," was the chairman's parting shot.

He snorted and nearly knocked his chair over as he got up, his nostrils flaring like a charging rhino. Had he been Caucasian his face would have been beet red. As he headed for the door I was on his heels, furious at him for being such a bully. I was determined to resolve our present tiff. When he entered his office I was right behind him, not giving him a chance to call Ms. Kalei to run interference.

"That was totally uncalled for. You've your role and I have mine. So, what is the problem?"

"You," the chairman spat out.

"You have been here for less than two weeks, much of which you've spent away from your office and all you've learnt is I'm the problem," I said as sarcastically as I could manage.

I had decided I was not going to take anymore gaff from the ruffian. I was not going to kowtow to this loutish novice.

"You are fired," he told me.

"Sorry, only the board can do that," I pointed out.

At that point I realized both of us were beginning to sound like spoilt brats, but I was still fuming so I left for my office.

As the situation stood, I would have had no choice but to quit. That afternoon I composed my letter to the board, giving its members the option of replacing our new chairman or accepting my offer to terminate my services at the end of the statutory two-month notice. I realized I could not ask the board to consider the option of retaining me without giving a full account of what led me to this drastic conclusion. Nevertheless, doing so would have been undiplomatic and would likely count against me in professional circles. Chances were that the board would not go against the prevailing political wind by firing the idle chairman in any case. It took the board only one week to accept my resignation.

The chairman and I have not spoken to each other since the day of the aborted meeting. Whenever we have had to communicate Ms. Kalei has conveyed the necessary information.

During the past several weeks I have been frantically looking for similar positions but have found none in the entire country. At the same time, I have noticed some of my old acquaintances have been avoiding me; perhaps they do not want the wrath that is being visited on me coming their way too. It is a month and a half after giving notice and I have reached the point when I'm convinced if I'm going to continue providing for my family I'll have to leave Kenya. This is a decision that I do not make lightly in view of my elderly parents. I'm uneasy that my financially less able younger brother has agreed to do the little he can for them. The worst though is not being able to tell my parents where and when I am going –I simply do not know. I am barely managing the dislocation my change of fortune is causing in my own family.

My wife, Sue, has been given a one-month notice even though she, too, has had glowing recommendations from her immediate supervisor. She was told the reason she was being let go was that the government was Africanizing her position. That she is a citizen of Kenya makes no difference. Essentially, I'm being paid back for standing up for what I believe to be fair. Apparently, stubbornness runs in the family; as they say, "I come by it honestly."

Three days ago I cleared my desk and office. It was my last day at work, an occasion that brought the rare tears in Ms. Kalei's eyes and several emotional farewells from other employees. "You're throwing us to the hyenas," one told me as I exited the brown brick building.

I expect little in way of severance pay. Any transitional or moving expenses will have to come from our meager savings, but somehow we will manage. We have to since we do not intend to burn all bridges and sell our home. In time, I expect to get some income from renting it out. We should vacate the house in about three weeks. Our friends in Canada -- relatives of my wife -- have invited us to stay with them and have offered to help us look for employment when we get there.

In the meantime, the laughter in our home has ceased. Long hours of worry, planning and fatigue, punctuated by flares of foul temper, have taken over. I hope this is but a passing phase and not a fatal blow to our marriage.

For the time being we are waiting for my wife to terminate her employment. As for me, being unemployed has given me time to ferry our children to and from their international school. Yesterday I ran into another parent, Dr. Moffett, who I met and immediately liked almost one year ago when I gave a speech on NGO's role in society at a conference in Lusaka, Zambia. Through him, I learnt the international organization he works for was looking for an independent person to do a survey on the efficacy of funding NGOs in Eastern Africa. He wondered whether I had anyone in mind I could recommend.

"I'll do one better. I've just resigned my position and would love to help you," I offered.

"I don't believe in luck, but the truth is, we were thinking of offering you enough inducement to lure you from your former position," Dr. Moffett beamed. "Can you come in tomorrow morning and we'll work out the details, if that's OK with you? Today, I'll give the chairman the good news."

"How about ten o'clock? You're still on Koinange Street?"

"Same old office. Agfa House, third floor. Here's my card. Look forward to working with you. See you tomorrow."

The thought of seeing that old building again, with its rounded corners and fading cream colors, put a spring into my walk. This was providence!

Last night I mentioned meeting Dr. Moffett to my wife

but left out the job offer. I did not know then what I know today. I will be working as an independent consultant, free to hire additional help if needed. Such help will not affect my fee (salary) which the organization has fixed at twice my previous salary. The survey final report becomes due in six months.

The best part is that Dr. Moffett's organization has deep pockets: it handles grants from several major, international philanthropic bodies whose main focus is sub-Saharan Africa. Judging from comments his chairman made, I may just have started what could turn out to be a successful and respectable consulting business. Our first business meeting is a week from today.

I can hardly wait to tell Sue the great news! Fortunately, we have not yet apprised our children of the big changes that were about to take place in their young lives, leaving their school and all their friends. Better yet, I will not have to worry about taking care of my parents or not seeing them whenever I so desire.

FIFTEEN

ALTHOUGH THE YOUNG generation from Kithongoto had spent its early years in the strict social structure of the church many from that group had gradually changed their lives as they went through their university studies or became employed away from the confines of their home community. The evangelical religion practiced in their home town strictly forbade drinking alcohol but their outlook had become more cosmopolitan and less fundamental in matters of religion. It was not unusual to find many of them socializing in bars or members-only sports clubs where alcoholic beverages, especially the locally brewed beers, were regularly served. Several had joined elitist golf clubs, such as Muthaiga, and were moving in the moneyed circles of the elite of the country.

Nyamai, Samuel and Nzungo were among the young Turks at Muthaiga Golf Club who regularly had a round of drinks together after their round of golf. Sometimes they hosted other Kithongoto young men of their generation at the club. On one such occasion Samuel and Nzungo had just finished playing against their guests and were reminiscing with them about Kithongoto.

"If there were a high school there we would have more people from our area going to university," one of them pointed out.

"You know the government isn't going to open a new school anywhere near Kithongoto anytime soon," Nzungo observed.

"What happened to the old spirit of 'pull yourself up by your own boot straps'? That's what *Mzee*[3] said," countered the second guest, referring to the self-help spirit that Kenyatta, the first president of Kenya, often espoused. He was often referred to as simply Mzee with a capital letter.

"Are you serious about organizing a *harambee*[4] to build a high school?" inquired Samuel. Although not a product of Kithongoto, he had come to be involved in its politics through Priscilla, his wife.

"And why not? Actually when you think about it, one person has spearheaded most of the work there, and he wasn't even born there! Just think of where some of us would be if the good reverend had not come around and stayed," the first guest said.

"Let's face it. The reverend isn't in any state to do much more. In fact, I dare say he has done more than anyone could have expected. The five of us should form an exploratory committee. My brother here," said the third guest, using the term often meant for close friends to address Dr. Nzungo

---

[3] Respectful reference to an old man
[4] Self-help or fundraising event

Itumo, "and I will approach the chief and see if we can get some land set aside for the school. I'm almost certain we'll need some funds for that."

"Are you talking through your beer?" Samuel asked.

"No man! This time, I'm dead serious. Does anyone here have any doubts about the viability of such a project?"

Not a single hand went up.

"Then the three of you will start organizing the first *harambee*" he said, as he stared at Samuel and the other two guests.

"A toast to Kithongoto High School," Samuel announced as he raised his beer mug.

"To Kithongoto High School," the rest chorused as they all raised their drinking glasses, not realizing the political miasma of behind the scenes intrigue into which they were stepping.

They all agreed to meet again after one month.

When Nzungo and his friend approached the location chief with the idea of building a school he was evasive and did not immediately embrace the project. Here were young men several years his junior hijacking part of his plan for political advancement: he had thought building a high school in his location would propel his career into becoming a Member of Parliament.

"Such an undertaking will need more resources than your group can raise, Doctor Itumo," the chief remarked condescendingly.

"One has to start somewhere," Nzungo countered. "All we need at this stage is a piece of land suitable for building a high school."

"Do you have ideas as to where you'd build if you had your choice?"

"The field beyond the shops out towards the dam would be perfect. There are no buildings there and the ground is level for athletic and games fields. I believe the government owns the land."

"I see you've done your homework! That land was set aside for a future agricultural station."

"But we already have one not three miles from there and the land around it is underutilized. Would it not be cheaper to expand the present station as need arises? Besides, we're asking for the use of public land for public benefit. The school will be a community undertaking and you'll agree with us that there's need for a local high school."

"Give me a week to consult my committee."

"Do you need us to attend the meeting?" Nzungo's friend asked.

"There's no need," said the chief, putting them off.

Of course they knew the chief had the authority to make decisions concerning the use of public land but did not wish to back the reluctant local politician into a corner. So they scheduled a second meeting just over a week later.

During the intervening week, word got to the Member of Parliament (MP) for the area that some people were planning to build a high school at Kithongoto. He was a person given to interjecting the big words of political rhetoric such as Progress and Education for Everyone in his conversations. Like all opportunistic politicians, he wanted recognition for the effort. He knew some of the people mentioned as planners, so he sent word to Samuel saying that as the area MP he expected to lead the *harambee* effort. However, the planners ingloriously ignored his wishes because they had little time for attention-grabbing politicians. They informed him he could contribute money or materials towards the project if he wished. Of course the chief got wind of this development. It helped him make up his mind to stall the work of the planners since he was the obvious choice to oppose the MP during the next elections.

The chief decided not to call his committee together as he was certain that some of the members were aligned with his future political opponent and were therefore likely to take actions that would benefit the MP. The chief sent word to Dr. Itumo postponing their scheduled meeting and suggested they meet after two more weeks. The appointed politician was now determined to reap any polling benefits he could garner from building a school in his location.

The Kithongoto High School building committee doubled as each of the original five co-opted a friend, resulting in a group that now counted an accountant, a structural engineer, a banker and a lawyer among its members. They held their first meeting on a Sunday afternoon under a tree in the grounds of the Senior Civil Servants Club, off Ngong Road in Nairobi. Even though they were all casually dressed and sat on the ground, their agenda was as formal as if it were in a boardroom. Up for discussion were only two items: land acquisition and fundraising.

The accountant, as chairman of the committee, declared the meeting open.

"There's no need to introduce anyone. We've known one another for years. So, Nzungo can bring us up to speed on how the meeting with the chief went," he said.

"We were going to hear his decision on Thursday but he postponed the meeting. Now he says he needs two more weeks to reach a decision about the land," Nzungo reported.

"It seems to me, someone got to the chief," the banker remarked.

"He's dragging his feet. Perhaps he's waiting for "a little something" for his troubles," Samuel suggested.

"No. I think it's more than that. I heard rumors he may want to challenge the area MP in the upcoming elections. Maybe he wants to be the organizer for this project so that he can claim he's done something for the community," the lawyer said.

"He has been chief for almost six years and all he's done is get fat," Nzungo said bitterly. "He's so absorbed in his own affairs I doubt he would see such a project through. Probably not in our lifetime."

"I know the owner of the stretch of land next to the public section. I may be able to talk him into selling it to us and we could use that instead of the government land," said the lawyer. "I'll be in Kithongoto this coming weekend. So, if it is OK with all of you, I'll have a word with him."

"Do you know whether he's in the chief's camp or the MP's?" asked the engineer. "I think knowing his allegiance or lack thereof would make our approach easier."

"From his comments, I doubt he carries water for either one of them," the lawyer said.

"OK then. That's a great idea! You can give us your report at our next meeting. Should you need our help in the meantime, you know how to get in touch," said the committee chairman. "What are the plans for fundraising?" he continued as he looked in Samuel's direction.

"So far we've received donations from some of you as well as from companies some of us are associated with. Our first *harambee* event is set for the first Saturday of next month," Samuel reported and then with a smile added, "It will include traditional dancing and speeches about the worthiness of the cause as well as the 'passing of the hat'. We expect all of you to attend with your pockets full of big ones. Our treasurer can give us details of how much we've collected."

"I'm happy to report that in a period of one month the Kithongoto High School Fund has received just over KShs.75,000 (seventy-five thousand Kenya shillings), money that is now earning interest at the rate of eight percent," the banker said.

They had envisioned the final cash outlay needed for the school to be ready for students to be about KShs. 500,000.

"It's a great beginning to which I'd like to contribute my design and building inspection expertise as a donation. I'm anxious to start as soon as we acquire the land," added the beaming engineer.

"That's a surprise we all greatly appreciate," said the chairman. "From all of us, 'thank you.' And now, any other business? If not, it's time for beer and a game of snooker or darts. And whoever loses buys the next round."

The seemingly light-hearted group got up, brushed off the dried grass from their backsides and headed into the clubhouse.

The lawyer's meeting with the landowner did not go as well as he had expected. There seemed to be some degree of hesitation regarding the sale. It was not until the owner mentioned that he had been approached by the area MP that the lawyer connected the dots. Apparently the MP was trying to undercut the chief by announcing that he, the elected politician, was in the process of building a high school in the location. Obviously, the chief was equally determined to build his school on the public land beyond the shops. These machinations left no room for a coordinated and cohesive community effort towards fulfilling the urgent need at Kithongoto. These two big talkers were just wasting the organizers' time; they were like two roosters fluffing their feathers for a fight which never occurs. It also meant if the young men organizing fundraisers were going to avoid interference from the local politicians they had to hold their meetings away from the location.

Such difficulties did not deter them as they exploited their business networks to get the needed funds and were able to offer the landowner enough on their second meeting. After some negotiating, he agreed to part with the parcel of land. Now they were set.

Throughout their endeavors they had deliberately left out the old preacher's family. Early in the planning, it was unanimously agreed that to involve e'Muthembwa's family would be poor form since the old man had done so much for the Kithongoto community.

A year after Samuel, Nzungo and their three friends came up with the idea of building a high school almost all the estimated funds had been realized, in spite of the chief's attempts to sabotage the *harambee* effort in any way he could. The engineer had paid an architect to help in designing and constructing the basic school buildings.

As expected, neither the area MP nor the location chief had progressed beyond empty promises and neither contributed a single cent to the project. Obviously, talk came cheap to the politicians.

SIXTEEN

OLD AGE HAD stopped Reverend e'Muthembwa from doing more than attend the occasional Sunday service. Now the patriarch of his father's family, the only surviving child, he was exceptionally fit for some-one of the old preacher's age: his mind was unusually clear and his wit just as sharp. He had been spared that stage in one's old age when things that happened years before become as clear as day and night while what occurred yesterday, today or a moment ago is as clear as mud.

He had witnessed the arrival of white missionaries, struggled through the introductory stages of Christianity in his tribal area and the concurrent colonizing of the country by the British, the latter being a development which he never fully understood. He had seen the arrival of political inde-pendence and the dreams to which it bore barren fruit because a few greedy politicians had appropriated resources of the country for their own personal aggrandizement instead of putting them to public good.

In his quiet voice and with a twinkle in his failing eyes, he was determined to pass on as much knowledge and wisdom about the old days to the younger generations, especially his grandchildren, as they would let him. It seemed to him the younger generations were always in a hurry to go somewhere, usually accomplishing little in their constant movement.

When not regaling his audience with his reminiscences, the preacher often talked about the finiteness of life on earth. He would often declare,

"I'm near the end of my journey on this earth. Any time now, the Lord will call me home to rest. 'I have fought a good fight, I have finished my course, I have kept the faith,'" – quoting from St. Paul's epistle to Timothy. He expected to "go away quietly" without anyone noticing that he had passed on, he would remind Kanini, his wife of many years.

Family members listening would nod deferentially, aware that other than his quotation from the Bible the old preacher was never heard to boast of his accomplishments. He was a humble man with a steely determination who believed one's actions speak louder than one's words. None could say that Reverend e'Muthembwa's work had not been the impetus that changed Kithongoto from a sleepy, backward, unknown village to a center of development in the larger district.

The end of his life on earth, as he had often suggested recently, came one night towards the end of the rainy season. He went to bed at his usual time, about nine o'clock, but never woke up. The previous afternoon he had complained of a slight headache which he attributed to changes in the weather, hardly enough warning to prepare his family for the sudden though anticipated end.

The pillar of Kithongoto was no more.

In keeping with his wishes, e'Muthembwa's family planned to hold a small, private and quiet funeral. The church committee, however, wanted a spectacle. In the end all agreed to have both: he was buried three days later in the church cemetery with only his immediate family and various members of the church committees in attendance. His protégé, the current minister at the Kithongoto church, conducted the service.

As agreed, the church members were to hold a general commemorative service at the Kithongoto church a few weeks after the funeral.

News of his passing spread like wild fire as parents in the preacher's old congregation notified their children who worked throughout Kenya. They, in turn, told others who had gone through Kithongoto elementary school. Many, especially among the second generation from the area, had the recently departed preacher to thank for showing them the way to a better life.

As soon as they got the news, the educated generation started organizing the memorial service as well as a separate post-burial wake the following day after the service. The latter was arranged ostensibly to cater for those who would be unable to attend the upcountry church service but, in truth, it was meant to provide an opportunity for the younger generation to celebrate the old preacher's life free of the constraints of church dictum. It was decided the gathering would be at Joseph and Sue's house in Nairobi.

The crowd that turned up for the commemoration was too large to be accommodated inside the church building. It was decided an open-air memorial would be appropriate, as no rain seemed imminent that day. A speaker's dais was set up and a temporary public announcement system rigged. Nearly a thousand people attended, many in tears. Some sat while others stood along the periphery of the gathering. Among the latter was a man in his late fifties or early sixties with thinning hair that was beginning to turn white. Dressed appropriately in a white shirt and a black jacket, the medium tall man blended with the rest of the crowd and was among those who arrived at the commemoration just before the ceremony started.

During the heavily attended commemorative service which included, two cabinet ministers, the area Member of Parliament and district commissioner, several people gave touching testimonies regarding e'Muthembwa's service and his influence in the community. Those from his church were the most touching. Among these was Kaveke, now in her late sixties and still beautiful. Dressed in a black and white polka-dot dress and a black head kerchief, she had outgrown her youthful shyness and now stood to address the crowd of over a thousand.

"Reverend e'Muthembwa was the first preacher who convinced me that being a Christian was the way to a better and happier life. I was not sure what kind of man he was when he arrived here, many years ago. For those old enough to remember, we had other preachers who left us for one reason or other. The reverend stayed to build this great church and make sure our young ones got an education. Can you imagine where this community would be if he had not brought the word of God to us? I know I would not have met my joy, my husband.

"Thank you God for sending us your servant, the Rev. Gideon e'Muthembwa." With tears welling in her eyes she sat down.

"He was a father to me," started Priscilla Katee, appropriately dressed in black pumps, a dark pleated skirt, a white blouse and a navy blue jacket, a perfect example of the modern woman from the city. "And I say this without diminishing the role my own parents played in my upbringing. The reverend stressed the importance of education for *all* children. He showed us by his own example that girls were not commodities to be sold to the highest bidder. He often encouraged me to persevere in my studies when I was ready to quit." Her voice broke.

Sitting near the front of the crowd, Samuel, her husband, nodded and mouthed,

'You can do it, love.'

Encouraged, she swallowed hard and continued,

"He opened a new life for me and for all of us who didn't think we could ever improve our lives. Having an education has opened the possibility for us to hold jobs that used to be open for foreigners only. Like many here today, I'm sure, my life would have been very different if e'Muthembwa had not come to live among us. The times are many when my husband has flippantly thanked 'the old preacher' for making it possible for us to meet. Today, on behalf of my entire family, I thank God and the reverend's family for sharing him with us.

"May his soul rest in peace."

The crowd murmured in chorus, "May his soul rest in peace."

The location chief was the last speaker on the program. As he rose to speak the graying man standing at the edge of the crowd turned and walked away quietly, the same way he had appeared. Throughout the service he had stood still with a pained expression on his face. He neither spoke to nor made eye contact with anyone.

The chief was in his late forties, an early convert of the late preacher and a beneficiary of e'Muthembwa's push for education for all the community's children. He fixed the assembled mass with his gaze and in his sure voice addressed them:

"I was barely knee high when he came. My cousin's uncle was the chief then. Today, we celebrate a man of God who not only spread the gospel but introduced modern ways of farming and yes, building too. Look at Kithongoto and compare our area with others around. Who has more schools, more modern houses? Who is doing better?

"We can thank Reverend e'Muthembwa for his leadership and be glad we knew and lived with him. He had the wherewithal to pursue lucrative careers on this earth but instead chose to live a life of scarcity in order to share God's word with us. Our lives are more comfortable and fulfilled today, our souls richer and we thank him for this. He was a man who disdained the construction of monuments in honor of people. This was in keeping with his humble belief that all are equal before God. Because of his activism African ministers in our location now perform all the functions of the Christian church which hitherto were previously the sole domain of white ministers. I'm sure his memory will live in our hearts and in the history of Kithongoto.

"I'd like to end by paraphrasing a quotation from the Bible that our dear departed mentor and friend often voiced. He fought a good fight, he finished his course and he kept the faith. That was his motto, his philosophy to the end of his life on this earth.

"Thank you for sharing him with us," he said as he acknowledged the late reverend's family.

The gathering sang one of e'Muthembwa's favorite hymns. Then the service closed with a prayer by the new preacher.

SEVENTEEN

J OE MUTUNGA AND Sue's home, a two-storey brick house
with a terracotta roof, was situated in the quiet outskirts of
the city. The cream white trim made the house stand out
among the lush tropical vegetation in the surrounding gardens that occupied the four-acre plot of land. The property
was surrounded by a gray, four-meter high cinder block wall,
topped with coiled barbed wire and covered on the inside by
tethered wild, flowering passion fruit vines and multi-colored
Bougainvillea flowers. One could not see the house from the
open metal gate. From there the paved stone driveway curved
round to the house giving one the feeling of driving into an
arboretum with manicured mini lawns separated by a variety
of tropical trees and shrubs, all of different heights. Near the
house meter-high tree roses, exuding distinct and pleasant
scents, festooned the driveway.

Away from the gate and to one side on the largest lawn
amongst the trees a long covered table had been set.

Individual smaller, round folding tables, each with at least four chairs around it, were arranged in a staggered pattern around the large, long table; a pattern that took advantage of the shade provided by the tall flame trees. Electric lights had been strung above on the shade trees, just in case the ceremony lasted beyond sunset. It was a perfect afternoon for reminiscing.

Snacks and drinks were arranged in different patterns on the covered long table. The variety of drinks rivaled the bar at the Norfolk hotel, one of best 'watering holes' in town, an obvious sign that not many teetotalers or staunch born-again Christians were expected to attend the festivities.

The main organizers had arrived around noon with tables and chairs. About three and a half hours later the catering van was there to set up the feast.

By four o'clock the first wave of guests began to arrive and by five the garden was humming with quiet conversations. Small clusters of old and new acquaintances, drinks in hand, were scattered around the garden, some standing, others seated at the small tables. There were about two hundred people, all people whose lives in one way or other had been influenced by the presence of the late Reverend e'Muthembwa. Among the gathered were Priscilla, the deacon's daughter and Samuel Kimweli, her husband; Nyamai and his wife, Ndoti; and Nzungo, son of the education committee chairman, as well as the hosts, Joseph and Sue. Children and minors had been entrusted to the care of ayahs or older relatives at a neighbor's home.

As the master-of-ceremonies, Nyamai, the late reverend's son-in-law, soon motioned for the gathering's attention.

"Thank you for your attention and for coming to

celebrate my late father-in-law's life. Welcome. In about ten minutes warm food will be ready on the long table in buffet style. Please serve yourselves. The main part of our after-noon will start in about thirty minutes."

A while later, Nyamai stood on a low platform placed near one end of the long table and, again, called the gathering to attention. By now the groups' mood was more animated, less somber. The strong drinks were doing their job.

"Alright over there! Quiet down. I hope everyone has had something to eat and my friend over there didn't eat as much as he used to when we were in boarding school."

A few eyes followed Nyamai's pointing finger as laughter drowned any objection his friend might have had. He waited until the laughter died down before continuing,

"Now we've come to the part of our program where all those who want to say a few words may do so. Don't worry, if you have a lot to say nobody is going to stop you. So, who is going first?"

A slightly built, tall man stirred from one of the small tables and stood up to explain how the old preacher had intervened when he needed school fees and his own family could not raise the funds. E'Muthembwa had contacted various officials and in the end secured a scholarship for the young man. The tall man was grateful for having known the late preacher.

Several others rose and spoke about the preacher, each recounting how his or her life was changed by the preacher's intervention, counsel or influence. Then Nzungo who had been sitting close to the master-of-ceremonies rose, cleared his throat and addressed Nyamai,

"What I have to say will take a little longer. So please

197

bear with me." He then mounted the "speaker's box," the low platform.

"For all of us who grew up in Kithongoto and I think that is nearly everyone here, there was one constant; Reverend e'Muthembwa's stories. When I was old enough to start attending the adult church services I remember that was the first thing that caught my attention, and every Sunday I looked forward to the next installment. I can spend the rest of the afternoon and evening telling those stories. I may not remember what the moral of each was but many of the stories stayed with me all these years. Therefore, in honor of the late reverend, let me tell you what I most frequently remember.

"I'd just completed my second term in high school and was home for the holidays. I was at a crossroads because I was not sure I wanted to go back after the holidays. I did not share my doubts with my father. Talk of quitting school would have caused steam to come out of his nostrils. You did not argue with him about the value of education, in fact you did not argue with him about anything unless you wanted a proper hiding. So when e'Muthembwa asked me how I was doing in school I thought if I opened up and related some of the torture I had to endure he might sympathize and suggest to my father that he enroll me in a different school. Or, better yet, tell me I did not have to continue going to school.

"So, come with me to Ngunyi Boys' School – with apologies to all old boys in the present company.

"Exactly two months after my fifteenth birthday, I arrived at Ngunyi boys' boarding high school. It was not long before other older boys warned me about the big run.

*"'You're so small you'll die come next term,'
one of them teased.*

"'Did you ever do any running at your previous school?' another asked.

"They never gave me time to say anything, for this was part of the routine hazing of first-year students at this particular school. Besides, the less I said the more the older boys ignored me and that was what I wanted. Less hazing meant a happier first term because by the second term freshmen were beyond this rite of passage.

"Other than the occasional squaring off with an older student, my introduction to high school was all I had expected it to be: new friends, new ideas and a feeling that I was accomplishing something beyond my previous intermediate school. I also gained weight and grew taller by a few more inches. The older students did not look as intimidating at the end of the term as they did at the beginning; they were just slightly bigger boys.

"We are now in the sixth week of our twelve-week second term and come Thursday next week every student in the school will have to run the marathon. The route we will follow is secret, in case someone devises shortcuts to avoid running the whole twenty-six plus miles – so older boys tell me.

"'What if I don't feel well on Thursday?' I ask one of these boys.

"'You have to be dead before you're excused from running,' he tells me as the other older boys give a knowing look.

"'Only real men can survive the marathon and you don't look like one,' another bigger boy sneers. Then they launch into a hyped-up re-telling of what happened when they ran the marathon the previous year.

"'Remember, Syengo was so stiff he could not even squat to do his business,' Mulatya offers to all of us. (I almost forgot to mention that we had squat-upon toilets in our school.)

"'Yeah, but you forget I had to carry you to class,' Syengo counters.

"'You liar! I'm the one who had to bring you your dinner and nurse you into your bed,' Mutiso says.

"'You were frothing at the mouth and did not even know the way to your own dorm,' Simba tells Syengo.

"At this point I realize they are only playing a game of one-up-man-ship and I am not going to get any new insight into the upcoming race. I walk away and let them continue with their game.

"It is a week later and at last the dreaded day has arrived. Immediately after breakfast, I notice that no one is making any more jokes about what will happen after classes this afternoon. Our classes are as normal as on any other day, after morning lessons we go to lunch and then return for afternoon classes. However, afternoon periods are shortened by fifteen minutes. Immediately following the last class we head for our dormitories. In ours we change into our normal athletics outfits, our red tops denoting our dorm color. Shortly thereafter,

*the whole school is summoned by a bell to a central
courtyard. This is the beginning and end point of
our marathon. I notice the teacher on duty this
week is absent. He is supposed to be here whenever
we assemble. Instead, the school headmaster is in
charge this afternoon. Next to him stands another
teacher.*

*"'As all of you know, today is Marathon Day,'
the headmaster bellows across the assembled two
hundred boys. 'The aim is to see which dorm out-
performs the others. Everyone is expected to participate. If you can walk, you're ready for this
activity. Anyone failing to take part without my
permission will face severe consequences. As usual,
members of the school staff will be stationed at
strategic points along the route. You must surren-
der your chit at each checkpoint or you'll be
disqualified,' he explains.*

*"At the same time I notice the other staff
member is handing to each dorm leader color-
coded, partially separated strips of Manila paper
matching our dorm colors. The headmaster continues,*

*"'I can't stress enough how important this
event is. If you're disqualified your dorm will also
be penalized.' He then stops for a moment and
looks at the other teacher who gives a nod. The
headmaster continues, 'Mr. Chubb has finished
distributing the chits. Make sure you have five. If
you need more raise your hand.'*

"No one raises a hand.

"'Mr. Chubb will give you directions to the

first checkpoint. When you hand in your first chit, that *teacher will direct you to the next checkpoint. Any questions?'*

"*There are none.*

"*'OK, everyone's ready. Wait for Mr. Chubb to give the start signal and good luck.'*

"*We all look at Mr. Chubb and at that moment I wonder how he came to get such a name. He is by no means chubby. By his physique he could be an army sergeant. I notice he has a starter's pistol in his right hand. He gives the whole student body a once over and starts,*

"*'From here you'll run past the west side of the hospital, past the cement warehouse to the main road towards Kisulini. At the third sharp turn in the road you'll find Mr. Sumba. When you give him your chit he'll give you directions to the next checkpoint. Alright,* ready...' Thwat, *the pistol goes off and we are off too, a mass of five different colors: blue, brown, green, red and yellow - all of us running barefoot. The time is 3:30 p.m.*

"*Less than a hundred yards from our starting point I encounter the first obstacle, a three-strand barbed wire fence. Pairs of runners help each other through, one holding up a strand of the wire while the other crawls through. As soon as each pair gets through they let the wire snap back with a low hum and the next pair has to decide who is going to hold first.*

"*In the spirit of competition I realize I cannot expect anyone to stand there and hold the wire, but a dorm mate is close by. I hold, he crawls through and holds the wire for me to do the same. We bound off, chasing after the leading group of runners, past the hospital, the cement warehouse and onto the main road. By now we are all spread out, each establishing his individual rhythm, each runner a few paces away from the next. I have fresh legs and I can keep up with the leading group's pace. Along the unpaved, corrugated road, I run where vehicular traffic has rutted the surface; I dare not use the sides where heaps of loose sand have been stacked by vehicle tires. That would slow me down. Six miles down the undulating and curving road I come to the first checkpoint. I know I am not the first to reach Mr. Sumba but I am sure that I am near the first fifteen or twenty. I give him my chit.*

"'From here you follow the path to the river. As you run make sure to keep that hill in front of you. The next checkpoint is across the river. Good luck,' he says as he waves me on.

"The path is more like a deer trail with thorny bushes on either side. I decide the surest way to get to the next checkpoint is to keep an eye out for the hill. Less than a mile into the brush I run into my next mishap; my bare foot steps on a three-inch, poisonous acacia thorn. Fortunately, the thorn does not go all the way into my foot or break. I am able to pull all of it out and continue running.

"Now my foot is throbbing and rivers of sweat are coursing down my face and back but I am not ready to disappoint my dorm mates. I run downhill toward the river, dodging thorny bushes, holes in

*the ground and any other unpleasantness lurking
underfoot. The far riverbank comes into view and I
accelerate to pass a few other students from other
dorms. Suddenly, there is a ten-foot drop to a rocky
riverbed in front of me. It appears as if hippos use
the only visible access to come and go from the
river. I slide on my butt to the water's edge.*

*"A quick assessment of the riverbed tells me it
could be too deep to cross safely at that point. So, I
look around some more and notice there is a series
of rocks about fifty yards upstream that I could use
as stepping-stones and head that way. Other
runners before me had come to the same conclusion and as a result the smooth round rocks are
now glistening with moisture. If I did not have to
jump from one to the next the dampness would
present no problem, but near midstream is the
widest leap and I am scared. I am alone and do not
know how to swim. 'Just grit your teeth and go for
it,' I tell myself.*

*"Just as I land on the last stone I slip but
manage to propel myself onto the far riverbank,
relieved that I did not fall into the river. I get up
and scamper up the bank. Fifty yards away where
the deer trail joins a well-trodden path is the
second checkpoint. I recognize Mr. Veeder, our
Math teacher and run up to hand him my slightly
wet chit.*

*"'Go straight up the hill until you come to the
agricultural station,' he instructs me. 'Then make a
left, almost north-west, and go past the two huts
and turn right. The next checkpoint is about twenty*

yards after that.' His explanation tells me that the third checkpoint is almost eight miles from here and that I have already run past the mid-point of the marathon. I am encouraged that I have made it so far. As I hesitate in my stride in order to thank him because he is my best teacher, Mr. Veeder quickly glances at my bleeding leg.

"'Is your knee alright?' he calls out, almost as an afterthought, as I pick up my pace. I look and notice that when I fell at the river I skinned my knee and blood has dripped almost down to my ankle. I figure it will soon stop, so I continue uphill. What a hill! It is so steep I doubt a truck could drive up that gradient. The loose gravel is murder on my bare toes and injured foot, especially when pebbles press at the point where the thorn pierced. Two hundred yards up, three, four and the gravel section comes to a merciful end; then the steepest part of the hill starts and continues for nearly three miles.

"By now I have stopped sweating and salt cakes my brow and forearms, my thighs and calves feel as if someone has gone over them with a two by four. I cannot tell whether my foot is still in pain or not, but when I glance down at it I can see it is by now swollen. The fortnightly fifteen-mile runs from my previous school to my parents' home come to mind; they reassure me that I can survive this marathon, even though all I can manage is an uncoordinated slow trot. I have not found any casualties on the route so far and I am determined not to be the first. I trudge on, past several boys

who by now are barely walking.

"The hill has become more manageable, it has leveled off considerably. I pick up my speed, if it can be called that, but several other older boys run past me. I am glad none of them has the energy to make sarcastic comments about my pace. They grimly keep pounding the ground with their bare feet as they run farther and farther ahead of me.

"All I can think of is harnessing my energy well enough to get back to school. I estimate I have been running and walking for almost two hours, but I can't be sure. 'Don't think! One foot after the other. Keep going, that's the only way you're going to make it,' my brain tells my body. I no longer care whether I come in first or last, all I want is to get back to school. I stumble upon Mr. Makwata. I made it to the third checkpoint! I am ready to hand over my chit.

"'You're doing well. About three quarters of the students have yet to reach this point,' he informs me as I stagger towards him. 'Go straight to the airport road, about three miles from here. Follow that road until you come to the sign for Ngunyi, then veer right and head back to school.'

"As he slowly gives his instructions, I am running in place and as soon as I hear the word 'school' I am off. Now I am energized, I have survived the worst part of the route. I know from there on it will be mostly downhill, then a flat bottom part with a bridge across the river and a sharp rise right at the end. I can do it. It is almost three hours since we set off.

"Just as I join the dirt road to the small rural airport a truck roars past, raising a blinding, choking cloud of dust. I stop to reduce my panting and lessen the amount of dirt I inhale, but soon pick up my pace. I am running on empty, my limbs numb and my brain focused on getting back to school. 'Breathe out as your foot hits the ground. Take long steps, that will give your legs less pain,' my brain counsels.

"Am I fainting or is the sun really setting? It is just the hill behind me casting its long haunting shadow down to the river. Soon, I realize running down a steep hill when one is tired is precarious: I have to lean backwards and measure each step, otherwise I will fall face down. It is like driving with the brakes on. I look behind me but no one is racing to overtake me, and in front I can barely make out the color of the runner's top.

"Then panic hits. I have just run past the third checkpoint and I am heading back to school with two unused chits. I must have missed a checkpoint, but where, I cannot remember. I decide it is too late in the run to change the outcome, so I continue. Soon I am at the bridge and standing at the other end is Mr. Chubb with his hand out for my fourth chit, which I hand over without slowing down. I can only hope that I will need the last one for the final check-in.

"A mile or two and the flat river valley comes to an abrupt end. It is less than a mile to the school but the steep hill makes it seem like miles upon miles. In my state it feels like the steepest section in

the entire route. A few yards up I notice several students behind me, some older boys trying to catch up with me, I suspect.

"Time to show them how it's done. As I quicken my pace I can hardly lift my feet off the ground; my skinned knee has long ago stopped bleeding but is ready to go on strike and my punctured foot has swollen to almost twice its normal size.

"I can sense the end of the marathon run for I know the school is just beyond that cluster of trees. Like a horse heading for the stable, I give it my all and before long I am jogging up the school drive towards the central courtyard where we assembled earlier in the day. On the way I pass two older boys limping along, so dehydrated that they are literally foaming at the mouth. As I approach the courtyard I notice Mr. Sumba is now sitting at a table with a row of small stacks of color-coded chits.

"'Give me your last chit,' he orders and I let out a big sigh of relief.

"The clock sitting next to his left elbow says it is 7:30 p.m. I am so stiff I can hardly walk the last few feet to my dorm. A quick rinse with cold water and I am ready to limp to the dining hall for supper, where I find those who arrived earlier eating quietly. When I sit down no one says a word and I join in the silence as other students trickle in. Other than the sound of cutlery striking plates, our normally rowdy dining hall could pass for a morgue. Nobody has the energy to talk about what just happened.

"We ran our cross country-steeplechase-marathon race yesterday. Today everyone is hobbling along, some with sticks like old men and others – stoically determined to show how tough they are – are trying to walk without limping. I am among the latter, but make sure I walk as little as possible and only when I really must. I intend to sleep all weekend in order to recover from the ordeal and I am sure I will not be alone.

"I am proud I completed the run and that my dorm came in first in the marathon this year but I don't think we should be subjected to such torture just to complete our schooling. I hope you agree with me, reverend. It was so bad, I'm thinking of not going back.

"The reverend listened patiently until I finished my story then asked,

"'How are you feeling today?'

"Fine," I said, somewhat put out by what I thought was a change of subject.

"'I'm glad to hear that. Then remember this: that which does not kill you strengthens you, my son.'

"After that I gritted my teeth and went back to school, but it took me several years to fully appreciate his advice. I'll forever be indebted to him for indirectly blocking the door before I bolted out to certain oblivion."

When Nzungo finished telling his story there were a few catcalls, some telling him he should go into preaching. For most of the people, though, tears were welling in their eyes. Joseph Mutunga's appearance on the platform got the crowd silent and expectant.

"We thank you all for coming to celebrate my father's

life and to mark the end of his work on this earth.

"Much of what I might say has already been said," he continued, his voice choking slightly. "Many of you know he could be demanding and yet attentive and kind. Above all I remember my father as loving and full of surprises. I remember when Sue and I went to see him for the first time. I was apprehensive. I expected him to rebuke me for wanting to marry outside the tribe but instead, my wife and I got a heart-warming blessing.

"Truly no one knew what to expect. None knew what his reaction to any situation was likely to be. One, however, could always be certain his response would be warm, considerate and given with love.

"It gives me enormous pleasure and satisfaction to hear the stories, to hear of the many ways in which my father helped shape your lives. I'm glad our family shared him with all of you.

"Thank you again for your presence here today."

Just as Joseph was sitting down Samuel was approaching the platform. According to Nyamai, this was an unexpected development, the late preacher's son was supposed to be the last speaker but a few words whispered in his ear made him smile and sit back. It seemed the gathering was in on a secret from which the late reverend's family had been kept.

"Joe and Esther, we all share in your loss. We all rejoice in having known your father. Even though I did not grow up in Kithongoto I have, through Priscilla, vicariously become acquainted with your late father's contribution. The truth is, without him I might never have met my dear wife. I know he hated being praised but he cannot stop us from remembering him, from cherishing the inestimable contribution he made to all our lives.

"We believe his life should be celebrated. Indeed, it should be commemorated. It is part of the history every Kithongoto child should know. To this end several of us got together and decided we are going to spearhead a drive to raise funds for the new King'ele High School at Kithongoto. For those of you who may not know, King'ele was the reverends given childhood name.

"We have already negotiated the land on which we are going to put up the buildings and a third of the funds we hope to raise are in the bank. We believe such a project would meet e'Muthembwa's approval and standards. We hope you, too, will agree with us and give this project your blessing.

"Thank you Sue and Joe for opening your home for our celebration."

EIGHTEEN

MUTUNGA AND SUE were recovering from the strain of all the activities since the death of his father and hosting the memorial two days earlier. Everything had gone as expected until the pleasant surprise about the high school to be built at Kithongoto. The best thing about it was that the planning committee had insisted Joseph and Sue not join but only allow the committee to proceed.

While the two were reminiscing about the wake, the guard at the gate to their home called with news that there was a man who wanted to see Mutunga but was unwilling to state his business. Mutunga was suspicious but chose to walk the short distance to the gate. At a distance of about twenty meters, the stranger standing outside the gate appeared well to do with patches of gray thinning hair showing above the white around his ears.

"I'm Mutunga. What can I do for you?" he addressed the stranger as he stood next to the guard.

"You don't recognize me, do you?" the stranger said as

he slightly gestured with his hands.

Something in the movement was familiar. Where had Mutunga seen it? He stared at his visitor, trying to remember where they had met. The visitor took a short step towards Mutunga but before he could take another the guard was standing between them. The visitor smiled,

"I'm glad you're quick," he said to the guard as his smile turned into a chuckle.

The smile and chuckle did it. The arms gesture was his father's and the smile so much reminded him of his mother. How could this be? His older brother did not resemble this man, as he recalled the brief encounter with him at the city center market. Still suspicious, Mutunga addressed the smiling visitor in an even tone,

"What's your name?"

"Matthew, your older brother."

"If that's true, tell me what's our mother's name and where was she born?"

"You're a difficult one to convince, aren't you? Kanini, daughter of Kithue, from Miambani and for good measure our sister's name is Ndoti."

The resemblances were mounting as the visitor talked. It was hard to believe but it became clear that this was actually his long lost brother! Mutunga motioned to the guard to step aside and extended his hand to his brother who took it and pulled him closer. They embraced with warmth that made up for the lost years.

"Come meet the rest of my family," Mutunga offered as he led his older brother up the driveway. "I still have some questions I need answered but they can wait until we sit down. By the way, how did you find me?"

"While you were at the university I knew where you

were but after that I lost track of your whereabouts. Then two weeks ago there was your picture in the *Daily Nation* accompanying the story about the NGO you work for, so I made some calls, talked to some people and got your home address!"

"I'm really glad you did. I've been trying to find you, too."

When he introduced his brother to Sue, she immediately noticed the similarity in the way each held his arms as well as the inflections in the way they talked. Still, Mutunga wanted an explanation about his experience at the market and one which Matthew was all too eager to give.

It was true that at one time he had sold wood carvings at the market but after his business got bigger he started an export business. He had left the market stall before his three-year license from the city council had expired and therefore had sub-let the stall to his friend, Kiendi Muthusi. That was the man Mutunga met and the one who did not give his real name for fear that the city supervisors might have been within hearing distance. The city did not countenance the practice of subletting stalls.

Matthew told his brother that for years while growing up he had been bitter about their father disowning him but when he married and became a father himself he came to appreciate the intense desire for one's children to get an education and better their lives. Remembering how badly he had behaved and how he had rejected all of his father's advice, he forgave him. He had not had an easy time with raising his own children and now understood part of the pain their father must have gone through. Matthew was proud of their father's dedication to his calling and chose to stay away because he did not want to embarrass the old man or cause a

215

scene. He also wished he had gotten in touch with his brother earlier but he needed to get his own house in order, get his business secure so that when he showed up Mutunga would not think he came only because he needed financial help.

As the two talked and shared early childhood memories, Matthew happened to mention that after inadvertently learning that their father had died he had surreptitiously attended his commemorative service at Kithongoto. After he heard the two women give their testimonials about their father he was so overwrought with emotions he left before the chief gave his speech. He had felt some of his old anger towards his father welling up in him and did not want to challenge his self-control by staying longer because he was not sure in the end he would win. Matthew wanted to be at peace with his father's soul.

Over the years Kanini had acquiesced to her husband's wishes that they not mention Matthew; that any thoughts about him did not jibe with Christianity. She understood her preacher husband's stand and respected his faith and desire to do good for the community but she never reconciled her maternal wishes with his stance. She knew to go against his wishes would cause a rift between them, a parting that would eventually destroy their marriage. Silently and steadily she stoically suffered the absence, indeed the loss, of her first born in order to safeguard her husband's calling. Kanini believed that to be a good Christian wife she had to be subordinate to her husband's mission.

She had lived with this belief for so long that even after his death she did not immediately start thinking of her first son. Besides, even if she were to find him she could not introduce him around Kithongoto without running the risk of tarnishing her late husband's reputation. Almost six decades later, what explanation could she come up with to satisfy those who would accuse her of going against her late husband? They had been married for so long that she had come to care about the preacher's legacy as much as he had treasured the success of the church.

Secondly, would her son want to be found after being shunned for so long? Her thoughts about Matthew remained unfocused, scattered to the point of inaction.

Before Matthew left his house, Mutunga had promised to broach the subject to their mother about getting reacquainted with her first son the next time he talked to her but he was not sure how to proceed. He wondered whether he should simply tell their mother he had seen his brother. Or, should he gradually bring up the topic with a view to eventually telling her about Matthew? He was sure that in some way or other he was going to re-introduce his brother to their mother for he had promised Matthew that much.

Recalling their mother's reaction many years ago when he had asked her about his brother, Mutunga remembered she seemed more afraid than annoyed that he had asked. He had never been sure what brought on the fear and did not have the will or desire to find out. The more he thought of the family dynamics the more he was certain that his mother was afraid of angering their father and this realization gave Mutunga hope that he would be able to talk his mother into meeting Matthew.

He did not have to wait for long as his mother decided to make the one and a half day trip by bus to visit him and Sue a month after Matthew came to their house. The loss of Kanini's husband had left her depressed as might be expected. Sue had insisted that meeting her first son would lift her spirits but Mutunga was not sure his mother was ready for the shock of seeing Matthew after nearly sixty years. He was spared having to make an immediate decision when he called his brother's house and learnt that Matthew was away on business for several weeks, so he chose to try to gauge his mother's reaction regarding a hypothetical meeting with her first son.

"Mom, do you remember when I was about five or six years old I asked you about my brother, Matthew?" Mutunga inquired tentatively as they sipped their tea.

"Yes," replied his inscrutable mother noncommittally.

"You never did tell me what happened. It must have been something awful because neither you nor dad ever talked about him."

"Yes. What he did does not bear repeating. That's water under the bridge and wherever he may be he's had to live with it," she responded in a hollow voice.

"Did you ever forgive him?" Mutunga asked calmly.

"It's between him and his god, if he has one, but I'll always be his mother," his mother answered flatly with an enigmatic expression on her face.

"Does that mean you would talk to him if you met him today?"

"Do I talk to the wind? That's a silly question since he's not here and I gave up the thought of ever finding him. I don't want to dwell on painful old memories. Let the past be."

Her tone had changed to chagrin although her years as a preacher's wife had taught her to keep her face impassive under pressure.

This whole exchange left Mutunga ambivalent as he could tell his mother was getting upset. Apparently the thought of Matthew still gave rise to very raw emotions in her. Perhaps it was the possibility that she may never see him again that prevented her from clearly admitting that she would want to speak to him. What if he told her that if she chose she could meet her adult first son?

Children can be thoughtless at times, thought his mother. The pain had never diminished: it remained wedded to her heart throughout the years. She had made a hard choice in order to support her mate when their son went astray but the rest of her children could not fill the void Matthew left. It was a high price to pay for the sake of the rest of the family. If only she could be certain the rest of his life had turned out well.

"Mother, I'm sorry for bringing this up but I have to know. It's important for me to know. If you can give me a straight answer I promise never to talk about it again. Please give me a yes or no. If it were possible, would you want to see Matthew again?"

Mutunga held his breath while he watched his mother's face go through various emotions: pain, remembering, hope, as she struggled to come up with an honest response. Could it be possible her son knew something about his brother that he was not letting on, she thought. She struggled to emerge from the long shadow of her late husband as her mother's affection took over. She tenderly replied,

"Yes. Very much," as her voice choked.

Mutunga got up quietly, put his arms around his

219

mother's shoulders and almost whispered,

"Thank you."

As promised he did not ask any more questions about his brother during the three and a half weeks their mother stayed at his house but he did not need to for the gate was now open for him to work out how he was going to get her and Matthew together.

Between his own work and Matthew's traveling it was difficult to find a time when he could get his mother to come for a visit. Soon it would be planting time and his mother would be busy supervising the field workers on her small farm. Two overseas meetings that had been scheduled for early November were suddenly cancelled and this gave Mutunga a month during which he could arrange a reunion if his brother was going to be around.

His apprehensive call to his brother's home brought joy for Matthew was going to be working from home for the next month or so. Now all that remained was for Mutunga to get in touch with their mother. Since she had no telephone, he sent word to her via people traveling to Kithongoto that he and Sue had a special event at their house they wanted Kanini to attend. He offered to go and fetch her if she was willing.

A day before the appointed day, a Saturday, Mutunga left work early to drive to his parents' home. He had decided not to say anything about the "special event" until the next day and fortunately, his mother did not press him to divulge any details about it. When he drove her to Nairobi on Saturday morning, Kanini was pleased Sue had set up her home for a party with various cooked and baked dishes and in deference to her mother-in-law's Christian beliefs had no alcoholic beverages on display. On noticing the decorated house Kanini cheerfully burst out,

"Am I the guest of honor?"

"Yes and no," her son replied fixing a steady gaze on her face.

"Stop talking nonsense! That's no answer," she shot back.

"Oh, you'll soon find out," Sue added with a smile. She had learnt to tease her mother-in-law in the same way Mutunga often did. The pair had arranged for Matthew to arrive a couple of hours after Mutunga returned with his mother and a quick telephone call confirmed that Matthew was planning to be on time. Now all they had to do was prepare Kanini for the moment.

"Mother, you remember a few months ago I was asking about Matthew? I *know*, I promised never to bring up the subject again," Mutunga observed.

"And now you break your word," his mother said accusingly.

"Yes, but with good reason. Several months ago he came here but I was not sure you ever wanted to see him again. When you told me you'd like to meet him we started working on such a meeting."

He paused to see how his mother was taking the news but her expression told Mutunga very little for she seemed to be in deep thought as she stared at an open window. With his and Sue's children away on a weekend camp the house was suddenly very quiet. Sue had been listening as she worked in the kitchen but had stopped working when her husband started talking about his brother.

"Did he look well? Where is he now?" Kanini asked, coming out of her deep thoughts.

"Yes he did. He's at his home in Eastleigh or somewhere in the city," Mutunga replied. "He should be here in about one and a half hours' time."

"That's the best news I've had in a long time," his mother declared as an almost imperceptible smile came to her otherwise somber face.

Simultaneously Mutunga and Sue let out a sigh of relief. The "old lady" was tougher than they had thought.